DRACULA
REBORN

Damian Woods

DEDICATION

Dedicated to the family and friends who have always
offered their advice, encouragement and support
throughout this whole endeavor.

CONTENTS

Acknowledgments   i

PART ONE

Chapter I   1

Chapter II   14

PART TWO

Chapter III   18

Chapter IV   32

Chapter V   41

Chapter VI   53

PART THREE

Chapter VII   59

Chapter VIII   84

Chapter IX   98

PART FOUR

Chapter X   115

Chapter XI   128

ACKNOWLEDGMENTS

I would like to acknowledge the works of Bram Stoker, creator of one of the greatest horror characters in all of fiction.

PART ONE

Chapter I

1897

6th November– Castle Dracula, the Carpathian Mountains

Dracula, the King Vampire, was dead.

Dusk settled over the castle courtyard like a blanket. After the chaos had ended, silence fell. The great earth-box, once the focus of all their collective energies, was now forgotten. Its previous occupant was now an ash-like pile of dust, a light grey against the dank, mouldy dirt inside. Next to it was the cart on which the earth-box once stood.

Leaning against its large, wooden wheel lay the lifeless body of Quincey Morris, skin as pale as the snow, but with a look of peaceful contentment on his still face.

Around him were his friends, all with their heads bowed in sadness and thanks for the heroic actions of their brave companion. Arthur Holmwood knelt on his friends left, trying to remain stern in the face of his sorrow. Jack Seward was on Quincey's right, holding his hand, willing life to enter his old friend once again. Jonathan and Mina Harker stood at Quincey's feet. Harker held his wife tightly. He looked down into her eyes, which sparkled with new tears, and then up toward her forehead, now free of the blemish that the vampire's curse had put upon her. He kissed it gently. Mina held him tighter.

Professor Abraham Van Helsing, the leader and driving force of the group and all their efforts to destroy Count Dracula was the first to speak.

"We must take care of our friend" he said solemnly.

As one they surged forward, lifting Quincey carefully and placing him on the carriage that Van Helsing had used to travel to the castle. The pool of blood beneath the body had already begun to freeze in the dropping temperature.

As they gazed upon his peaceful face, they reflected upon their long journey together, starting almost a year ago, with Jonathan's torturous ordeal at the hands of the vampire, inside Castle Dracula itself. As a Solicitor, he had acquired property for the Count in London- Carfax Abbey and an old house in Piccadilly. He had been sent to Transylvania to get his signature. There he faced weeks of unimaginable torment, but the hope and desire to return to his fiancé (now wife) had driven him on and spurned his escape. This was followed by Mina's dear friend and Arthur's fiancé, Lucy Westenra, being infected by the vampire's curse in Whitby, the port where Dracula's ship had landed.

Dracula had planned to launch a campaign to spread his vile disease across the country, and then perhaps, the world. London would have been its centre. He could bend the minds of the weak to his will and use them as his minions.

Doctor Jack Seward had become involved at that juncture. As the Head of an Insane Asylum, Jack had treated R. M. Renfield, a curious madman who, they found to their cost, was in the control of the Count. Professor Van Helsing, Jack's former teacher, had then entered the fray. As a student of the occult he had helped identify the mysterious ailments which had befallen Lucy. And finally, Quincey Morris, lifelong friend to Arthur and Jack, had joined the circle of friends who had been affected by Dracula's vile presence. Lucy's true death and salvation had bonded them all ever closer, while Mina's infection by the Count had solidified them into a force of unstoppable good. It was as if each of them was a single piece of a stronger whole.

Mina covered Quincey with one of the furs.

"Our efforts have cost us dear," continued the Professor "but we can rest easy knowing that Mina is safe, and the evil destroyed. And our dear Quincey's soul is secure in heaven."

As if in answer, stars began to appear in the darkening sky, blinking like diamonds.

"We must go," said Arthur, wiping the now stiff trails of tears from his face. "It is still dangerous here. There are wolves to contend with, and the paths may be difficult to pass in the snow."

"Arthur is right." Van Helsing said, nodding. "Come."

They began to gather their things and collect the horses, who had wandered away in the confusion and battle with the Szgany gypsies.

Above them, on a rocky outcropping, those same gypsies watched.

Overwhelmed by the severity and fierceness of the foreigner's attack, the Szgany had quickly retreated, all promises and vows holding them to their master's defence forgotten. They had seen one of the men, the one with the woman, slash wickedly at Dracula's throat with a kukri knife. They saw another – the one lying dead, plunge a knife into their master's chest. That one at least had had revenge brought down upon him. One of the Szgany had delivered the killing blow. They watched the foreigners now, from behind large boulders and gnarled trees. They saw them gathering their things and leaving. When they had finally disappeared out of sight, the Szgany came out from their hiding places and walked back into the courtyard.

Above them, the castle battlements loomed. The spires looked like crooked fingers, reaching up into the sky. Night was almost fully upon them.

They approached the earth-box cautiously. They had seen Dracula turn to dust, but gypsies are superstitious, and the idea that the Count's vengeful spirit may remain to taunt and torture them, filled their hearts with fear. They knew that they had abandoned him in his most desperate need, so dishonour compelled them at least to conceal the earth-box in the castle, away from the elements.

Two of the Szgany approached the castle doors as others lit torches. They pushed and shoved at the ancient wood, then began attacking the old and rusty lock with their knives. It seemed an age until the metal screeched, as if in awful pain, and the massive doors creaked open. The others warily approached the box. They lifted the wooden lid and put it back in place. With another huge effort, they all lifted the heavy box inside, dumping it in the entrance way. The castle stones were stark and cold and the feeling of emptiness heavy, like a chain around their necks.

Unsure of how else to serve their master, they walked back out into the snow, closing the doors behind them with an ominous thud, leaving all to the welcoming embrace of the dark.

6ᵗʰ November – Durham, England

Alexander Frye paced back and forth in his cell, wailing and crying. He clung to the side of his head, looking about the floor like he had lost something precious and irreplaceable. Occasionally, he would fling himself against the padded walls, clawing at them, before pressing his tear-strewn face into the protective material.

At the cell-door, the Attendants watched through the small hatch. Simons, the Head Attendant, had decided not to enter the cell with a straight jacket yet. Despite the violence of his actions, Frye had not caused any damage to himself or anything else. Simons felt that whatever was causing the episode, would pass sooner rather than later, and if Frye's body were to be confined now, he would only get worse.

He had been trying to talk Frye down over

the last half an hour. His words were calm and his tone soothing, but Frye had not responded to him in any way.

"Come on, Frye," Simons said. "Why not rest yourself on your cot a while, ay?"

Frye gave no sign that he had heard.

"Gone!" he screamed. "The Master has gone!" He started to wail again.

Dr Ludlow approached the cell. The other Attendants parted so that Ludlow could get a look though the hatch. "Any change?" he asked Simons.

Simons shook his head.

Dr Ludlow peered through the opening, adjusting his gold-rimmed glasses to keep everything in focus.

"He was here. He was here!" squealed Frye, jabbing his forehead with his finger like an angry woodpecker.

Ludlow stepped back from the hatch and pursed his lips. "Open the door."

Simons nodded. He took out the large iron keys which jangled heavily in his hands. He unlocked the door and opened it.

"I don't think he'll try anything, but be ready nonetheless," Ludlow ordered as he entered the cell.

Frye was still pacing.

"Hello, Alexander. It's Dr Ludlow."

Frye did not look up. "He has gone." he said flatly.

"Who has gone?" Ludlow asked, gently.

"They have killed him. The Master said they would try. But he was supposed to kill them. He said he would."

"Who has been killed, Alexander?" Ludlow queried.

Frye's neck snapped back like a striking snake, seeing and hearing the Doctor as if for the first time. He began to move quickly toward him. Ludlow braced himself, while Simons and the other Attendants began to dart forward. Suddenly, Frye fell at Ludlow's feet, as if begging. Ludlow gestured behind him for Simons and the others to come no further.

"They have taken him away," sobbed Frye. "Those filthy fools! But he told me. He told me about all of them."

Ludlow had heard Frye talking about the 'Master' before. Whoever Frye thought the Master was, he revered him and worshipped him greatly. Ludlow had begun to think that Frye had manifested in his mind a kind of 'god' figure. Despite many sessions and vigorous questions, Frye had never revealed much else, only that the Master would look after him and lead him to 'glory'. It had kept him calm somewhat, Ludlow thought, until the last week or so when he had started to become more agitated. The fact that Frye had now produced in his mind 'god-killers' was a very strange phenomenon. He didn't know how to feel about it. It could very well lead to a further breakdown in Frye's behaviour. Or it could even be his way of trying to kill off whatever it was in his mind that had caused his confinement in the asylum in the first place. The next weeks and months would be crucial in Frye's treatment, Ludlow thought.

Frye had curled up at the Doctor's feet. He had quietened down but was still whimpering feebly.

"Come now, Alexander. Up onto your cot."

The Doctor gestured for the Attendants to help Frye onto his bed. Frye offered no resistance. He was wiry and light, but all present knew how strong he was. He lay on his side like a toddler.

"He has told me what to do" he said, quietly. "He has asked me to help him."

"Has he?" said Ludlow, leaning down toward Frye. "What has he asked you to do?"

Frye gave Ludlow direct eye contact for the first time since the Doctor had entered his cell.

"Find him," he said.

Chapter II

21st November - Sailing back to England

They were all exhausted, physically and mentally. The stress and strain of the whole adventure into hell had lifted, but it had left dark fragments, like glass, seeping through their blood. Mina still experienced dreadful dreams, which would pierce her sleep. Jonathan remained by her side, ever vigilant. All he wanted to do was reach into her mind and take her troubles away, dropping them into the vast ocean. Van Helsing and Seward were always on hand to help where they could, doing their best to settle Mina back into a hopefully dreamless sleep.

Arthur, now Lord Godalming, walked the deck of the ship, as if on constant watch, as Quincey would have done. It all seemed so unreal that the nightmare was over. It was like none of them could trust in the finality they saw, when Dracula's body turned to dust. Jack walked with Arthur a lot; their handsome faces now drawn with lines of grief.

They talked of Quincey, of old hunting stories, of their adventures together. It helped to think of the good times, and to hope for good times to come.

23rd November

It was early morning, very cold and the waters were choppy as the ship neared Dover. They all stood on the deck together, looking out toward home. Toward safety. And hopefully, toward peace.

As the freezing wind stung their cheeks, Van Helsing turned to face them.

"I know not if this will ever truly leave us,"

he said. "but we cannot let our pasts determine our future or our fate, yet the lessons we have learned and the friendships we have made will stay with us forever."

They all smiled, solemnly.

"I would like for us to make a pledge" he continued.

"Anything, Professor," replied Arthur.

"Of course," said Mina and Jonathan in unison.

Jack nodded.

As the Professor began to speak, he looked at each of them in turn.

"We are joined together, so much closer than even blood can make us. No matter how far we may be away from each-other, should any one of us be in trouble, we must all promise to help." He held out his hand. "That is our pledge."

They all shook his hand in turn, promising with all their hearts to do as Van Helsing had asked. It was only Mina, who, instead of shaking his hand, brought it to her lips and kissed it.

Van Helsing smiled heartily and happily. Some playfulness had returned to his solemn face. "The rest of our lives are waiting for us," he said. "Let us do what we can to make them happy ones."

Above them, the sound of seagulls called them all home.

PART TWO

Chapter III

1901

2ⁿᵈ July

Alexander Frye sat across from Dr Ludlow in the small, cramped office. A single trail of sweat trickled down his brow as he waited for the old man to start speaking.

Ludlow was wiping the lens of his glasses with his handkerchief, taking an age to check their cleanliness before putting them back on his face.

Frye thought he was doing it on purpose, to make him uncomfortable. To test his resolve and patience. He gripped the sides of his chair until his knuckles went white, thankful that they were below Ludlow's line of sight, covered as they were by his large oak desk.

Dr Ludlow rested his elbows on the desk and thatched his fingers.

"You have been doing well, Alexander" said Ludlow, finally.

"Thank you, Doctor," said Frye, almost choking on each word. He wanted to throw them back in the Doctors face.

"Your progress has been superb, and you are to be congratulated." Ludlow smiled.

Frye smiled in return. "All thanks to your help, Dr Ludlow."

Frye's heart was pounding. He thought it was going to push through his ribcage and out of his chest. Over the past months, Frye's self-control had been due to a gargantuan effort on his part. His mind was focused on but one goal, to help his Master, and to do that he would have to be released from the asylum. Whether that was possible depended on the next words out of Ludlow's mouth.

"As you may know, Alexander, I am retiring soon."

Frye nodded, willing the man to get to the point.

"And before I go, I wanted to pass on some good news," Ludlow said, smiling at Frye as he would a toddler.

"Oh?" said Frye, feigning surprise. "What news, Doctor?"

Ludlow leant forward in his chair. "You are to be released."

Frye grinned.

...

1904

3rd September – London

Mina woke with a start. She bolted upright in bed and stifled a small cry. She was breathing heavily and a thin sheen of sweat covered her brow. Beside her, Jonathan stirred. Accustomed now to his wife's nightly terrors, his eyes opened, and he rested a caring hand on her shoulder.

"Are you alright?" he said, gently.

"Yes. Yes. It's just… the same thing," she replied, trying to wave it away.

She lay back slowly, into his arms. He held her close into a protective embrace, whispering words of comfort and willing her back to a restful sleep. After about ten minutes, Mina was sleeping softly, her rhythmic breathing suggesting, at last, a semblance of peace.

The nightmares had been constant since they returned home from Transylvania. Red eyes peering from the murky dark. Hands sprouting from the ground, trying to grab Mina and pull her down into the mouldy soil. Van Helsing had tried his absolute best to help banish the horrifying visions from her mind, but even he was powerless. He was forced to admit, finally, that they were the dark remnants of her traumatic experience under the evil influence of the Count.

Jonathan slid quietly out of bed. He sat on the edge, looking at his sleeping wife. He felt so utterly helpless in this. Mina had been so strong – maybe the strongest of them all - through their whole experience and now she had to use all her strength to fight off these nightmares. Nightmares he hoped would fade in time, though after almost six years, that seemed unlikely.

The one light they both had was their son. Quincey Arthur Abraham Jack Harker. A mouthful indeed, but they both just called him Quincey. In just over two months, it was to be Quincey's sixth birthday – the same day as his namesake died. Mina, he knew, held the belief that some of Quincey Morris's fearless and adventurous spirit had passed into their son and Jonathan had to concede she was probably right. The boy was a bundle of energy and happiness, who would charge first into any new situation. His face would crease into seriousness when faced with something he didn't understand, then quickly burst into joyful laughter at the slightest provocation.

Van Helsing had suggested, on the seventh anniversary of the Counts demise, that they should all travel back to Transylvania and go over the old ground of their most terrible of adventures. He had suggested that, now the land was free of the Count's evil influence, it might help Mina overcome her nightmares. The Professor had never been happy that he could not adequately explain her predicament and continued to search for a solution. Arthur and Jack agreed immediately. Anything that could help. Jonathan, however, was a little uneasy. He had no clue how going back there could help Mina, but Van Helsing had never steered them wrong, so he had agreed. Little Quincey would accompany them. His first overseas trip. He was still too young to be told everything that had happened – though Jonathan had often thought that it was something he should never be told- but a trip with his parents and extended family sounded an excellent idea.

Quincey would be up soon. Jonathan liked to spend as much time with his son as possible. His life as a Solicitor had grown expansively and he was happy that the occasional long hours at least allowed him to provide for his family, and the time he had with them both was very special. Sitting his son on his knee and asking him 'what would you like to do today?' had led to many escapades, at the park, at the zoo or even just playing hide and seek. Quincey's laughter was like a ray of golden sunlight shining on his face.

If only he could calm his wife's mind.

13th September– Cornwall, England

Alexander Frye sat in the corner of the small public house. Most of the customers were fishermen, and they were scattered around in small groups, or stood up at the bar, talking loudly about their latest catch, or about the weather, or sharing old stories of storms and wrecks past.

Frye was the odd one out. He was quiet and brooding. The Landlord looked on him unfavourably, as he had been cradling the same pint for half an hour.

Frye was thinking of the past. Of everything that had led him to that point. Time in the asylum meant nothing and everything all at once. Days could drag like walking through tar. Weeks and months could pass in a haze, drugged and senseless, barely knowing the difference between night and day. Frye had lived that way for more than a year after losing connection to the Count, his Master. His moods had gotten more desperate, more violent, as he sought to find that voice again.

Dr Ludlow feared that Frye would never come out of it.

It was Frye himself who realised, that if he wanted to help the Count, he would have to be calm, collected and patient. He *knew* he was sane. He always knew. His contact with the Master was real, but it was pointless to try and convince anyone else of that. Dr Ludlow would not understand. He would only treat him even more like an insane man, and keep him locked up, probably forever.

Frye could not allow that.

He knew he would at least have to act how Ludlow and the attendants expected a sane man to act. It would be no easy task. His drive to help the Count was hard to control. Frye wanted to get out of the asylum, and to stay out. He could have tried escaping, of course, but should he have been caught, his task, his duty, may never be performed. He would have to remain and be quiet and demure. He would have to listen and follow instructions and rules.

And worse yet, he would have to acquiesce with Dr Ludlow's wishes and agree that his Master didn't exist and was just a voice in his head. The very idea made him angry and it was anger that sometimes he could not conceal. It had taken a further three years of being supplicant and obedient, like a dog, before Ludlow deemed him fit for release.

Feigning happiness for being 'cured' almost made him sick, but thankfully, the genuine happiness he felt at being free to do his work made it easier. As he walked away from the asylum, Frye looked back up at the stark, cold building. Four years wasted, he thought. He would have to somehow make up the time.

It was not easy.

He considered going to London and trying to locate those who had killed his Master. He thought of killing them himself, but then decided no, Dracula would probably want that honour.

He had to get there. To Transylvania. But then came the other consideration, almost as important.

Money.

He travelled north at first, into Northumberland, then into Scotland. He felt it was best to go somewhere new. Working small, menial jobs was enough at first – the minute wages enough to maybe rent a room for short periods. The rooms were always dank and dusty, with peeling, cracked walls. But he could stomach it. After the asylum, he could stomach almost anything, until it dawned on him that the money he was making was nowhere near enough. Not for the journey ahead.

He started to travel again. Back south.

He was wandering through one of many forests. Around Blyth, he thought. It was deathly cold, and the path was strewn with decaying leaves. He had his head down, following a crooked pathway, nothing on his mind but his mission, his purpose. All else was secondary. It was early evening, and the birds had stopped singing. Apart from his own footsteps, trailing through the dead foliage, there was no other sound.

Then he felt a change in the air, and sensed movement ahead of him.

He stopped.

Two figures emerged from the dense trees, like they had sprung out of the ground itself. They were dirty and unkempt, with grizzled, grimy faces. One of them had a knife. The man started speaking. Frye didn't hear the words, so insignificant were they, but he knew exactly what the man wanted. He wanted his money and possessions – anything of value. Strangely, a calm settled over Frye at that moment.

He came to a simple conclusion, as quickly and easily as one breath follows another.

Murder.

He would kill to get what he wanted.

And these would be the first.

Frye screamed like a wild animal and lunged forward at the man as if he had springs on the soles of his feet. The man staggered back, completely shocked at this sudden, ferocious attack. Within seconds, Frye had wrestled the man to the floor and pried the knife from his hands. With glorious exultation, he thrust the blade into the man once, twice, three times, until an awful gurgling escaped from the man's throat. In a few more seconds, that sound ceased. The robber's companion had been too afraid to help and was starting to run away, but he slipped on the rotting leaves. Looking back, he saw Frye run toward him. He started screaming *no* as Frye raised the blood-stained knife and began stabbing over, and over, and over again.

When it was done, Alexander Frye leaned back on his haunches, heaving a sigh of pleasure. The murder had brought him a sense of relief and calm he had not felt since the last time he heard his masters voice.

Afterward, he searched though their belongings and found money and jewellery obviously stolen from other unlucky travellers. He took it all, smiling and laughing as he emptied their pockets and filled his own.

He had murdered many times since then – wandering, lonely travellers, each death bringing him closer to his goal. He made sure to continue travelling, this way and that, with no rhyme or reason, in case anyone out there was trying to capture him – the elusive killer…

…

As he sat in the public house, he smiled to himself.

It was time. He would stay a little longer in Cornwall, then move on.

Finally, he decided to order another drink.

Chapter IV

22nd September – Bistritz

Jonathan sat alone, looking out of the train window. Looking at the hills, fields and mountains he had seen twice before, but now, since the Count had died, it was like he was looking at them with new eyes, free from a shadow. They were truly beautiful. The sun cast a golden glow upon the entire landscape. Mina was asleep in their cabin. Her nightly terrors catching up on her still. Arthur and Jack were sat a little further down in the carriage, talking and smoking. Their easy laughter pulled Jonathan's gaze away from the window and toward them. He marvelled at them both, that they had been so lucky in wives as him, that would let them leave home and travel so far with friends on a mission that they neither could, nor would want to tell them all the details about. Arthur had married a wonderful lady named Laura. Kind and gentle, she had soothed Arthur's troubles after losing Lucy. Jack had met Stephanie, who was a wonderfully bright presence anywhere she went. The occasions of their weddings were times of happiness and celebration for them all.

Jonathan turned his head across the aisle to see Van Helsing, asleep, head lolling from side to side with the rhythm of the train. Lying next to him, with his head upon the Professors knee, was Quincey, his dark brown hair covering his eyes, also sound asleep. Jonathan smiled. He was unsure who had worn who out. Quincey had been a ball of energy since the trip began. They had seen dolphins during their short time on the ship. In truth, all their hearts had lifted watching the magnificent creatures gliding both above and beneath the waves, but Quincey had been completely enraptured at the sight. Mina's eyes had glistened with tears of joy. Since transferring to the train, Van Helsing and Mina had been teaching him – reading, writing and math, to make sure he didn't fall behind on his schooling.

"A smart boy you have there", Van Helsing had remarked.

Jonathan's chest could not help but swell with pride.

In between the lessons, however, Quincey, encouraged in no small part by the Professor himself, had become a wicked prankster, leading them all a merry dance and causing no end of laughter.

The train began to slow as their stop neared. They were moving on to the *Golden Krone Hotel,* another place Jonathan knew from his past travels. He had the landlady to thank for gifting the crucifix that had been his sole protection whilst at Castle Dracula. He hoped she would still be there, just so he

could look into her eyes and smile. He knew
they would all be comfortable at the Inn,
before moving on to the Borgo Pass.

23rd September- Dover

Alexander Frye had spoken to several
Shipping Agents before being told that one
ship, the *Elisabeta*, had already sailed to
Varna two weeks prior, but another ship was
expected soon. Frye wanted to rip out the
man's throat there and then. His weaselly
little face was making Frye twitch with
annoyance but he regained his composure.
No amount of money could make a ship
move faster, so he had no choice, yet again,
but to wait. He trudged away from the
offices, on the hunt for a small guesthouse.

24th September – The Borgo Pass

They travelled in two carriages, hired from
the Innkeeper. Jonathan, Mina and Quincey
in one, Van Helsing, Jack and Arthur in the
other. It was early morning and the sun had
touched the wisps of cloud in the sky with
golden edges. Jonathan drove the carriage

well, while Quincey sat up and rode with him, looking wide-eyed at the surrounding countryside. It had been Quincey, that morning, asking his father 'what are we going to do today?' He had become incredibly excited at the prospect of seeing a real-life castle. Mina sat in the back, looking out of the small windows. The last time she had travelled here, the Count's influence was upon her. Those memories seemed like a haze and she was looking at the countryside afresh. Her heart lifted. She began to realize, perhaps, that yes, the Count was truly gone. And maybe, with that realisation, would come peace.

Then, in the distance, she saw the castle.

It was standing as she remembered, as a cold monument to his evil. She shuddered. Quincey cried out in amazement at the sight, having never seen anything like it before. He looked up at his father and exclaimed that it was like something out of a fairy-tale. Jonathan's face tightened. He smiled back at his son so as not to betray his feelings. A fairy-tale? Yes, but it would have been a fairy-tale from the depths of hell. Each would react in their own way, he knew, but the only one he was concerned about was Mina.

Arthur and Jack stared at the great structure – the birthplace of all the evil that had changed their lives so completely.

The carriages pulled into the courtyard, the horses hooves clacking and echoing upon the stone covered ground. They wound the horse's reins around some broken branches, in case they should be spooked, and the carriages damaged or lost.

Jonathan helped Quincey down first. Arthur and Jack hurried to their sides.

"Come on, Quincey, let's go explore!" said Jack excitedly. He eyed Jonathan, that one look telling him that he would keep the young boy occupied should anything happen with Mina – though what that might be, none of them could say. Quincey took Jack's hand and they skipped off further into the courtyard. Arthur laid a reassuring hand upon Jonathan's shoulder, both men giving each-other a slight nod, before he too joined Jack and Quincey.

"Come on, Uncle Arthur!" shouted the boy happily.

"Give an old man a chance" replied Arthur, good humouredly.

Van Helsing merely waited, about seven steps back as Jonathan helped his wife down from the carriage. Her eyes immediately looked for her son.

"Be good for Jack and Arthur!" she called.

"I will, mother" he bellowed back.

She watched them a few moments more, rummaging around the fallen stones. She couldn't help but notice how the men would steal the occasional look at the castle, before looking away again, afraid perhaps that the building itself would come alive and try to harm them in some way. Finally, Mina herself looked fully upon Castle Dracula.

She seemed suddenly lost in the memory of it.

"Mina are you alright?" asked her husband. His kind eyes stared intently at her.

She didn't respond, only started to walk forward toward the huge, wooden doorway.

"Mina…?" said Jonathan again, concerned.

Van Helsing appeared at his side in an instant.

"Professor, what's the matter with her?" he asked.

"Give her a moment" Van Helsing said.

Jonathan looked back at her. She looked totally alone, dwarfed by the huge stone structure. He started to fear she would suddenly be enveloped completely by it. Seconds felt like hours.

She turned back toward them.

"It's… empty" she said.

Jonathan was confused. "Mina?"

She walked back up to him, placing her hands upon his chest. "It's empty. The whole place. Everything. There is... nothing here. I was expecting to feel... something. I don't know what. A presence of some kind, but there is nothing here that can hurt me, or any of us. He has truly gone." She smiled, such a smile of radiance it could equal the brightness of the sun. They embraced tightly.

"He's gone" she repeated.

"Yes," replied Jonathan, smiling. "He's gone."

He felt then, that when they journeyed home, maybe a new and happier life for the family was waiting.

Chapter V

19th November - Bistritz

The Station Master looked at Alexander Frye with a suspicious eye. Several foreigners had just left, and they all seemed cheerful and pleasant enough. This man, he pondered, had an unpleasant air about him. His clothes looked unkempt, and his head moved with odd, darting motions, like he was being stung by unseen insects.

Frye had not particularly enjoyed the sea crossing. The waves had been large and rolling, with white frothy edges that broke violently against the sides of the ship. His mood was now being made worse by this stuffy little man.

The Station Master could speak a little English, but he did not feel like helping the strange individual. Frye tried his best to pantomime what he wanted- horses, a carriage and directions to Castle Dracula. It was this last request that finally decided, for the Station Master, that he wanted nothing at all to do with Alexander Frye. He turned away from him with a non-committal shrug.

Frye was beginning to get angry. His eyes burned into the back of the Station Masters head before he too looked away, trying to find a solution to his problem.

It was then he spied the man, watching him. Dressed in strange attire – large boots, a thick leather belt with a huge brass buckle and a fur jacket. The man's eyes were piercing. Most people would turn away from such a gaze. Frye walked toward it. He stopped about three feet from the man, surveying him like a hungry wolf.

"Castle Dracula?" Frye said inquiringly.

"Dracula," the man replied, in a flat

monotone.

Frye had expected something like this may occur – that he may have to bribe to get what he wanted. While he had pawned most of the jewellery he had accumulated for cash, he had also kept some of it behind. He dug into his bag and brought out some gold rings and necklaces, showing them to the man, who was probably a gypsy, he thought.

The moment he saw them, the man smiled, nodding approvingly.

"Dracula," he said again, this time with a note of cheer in his voice.

The gypsy beckoned Frye over to his cart and two large, shaggy horses which Frye presumed, correctly, the man used to transport various goods about the countryside. He looked at Frye expectantly. Frye nodded at him, then handed over the jewellery, sealing their almost silent deal. They both clambered upon the cart. The man shook the reins and the horses moved off.

It was midday. Frye had no idea how long it would take to get to the castle, hours or days, he didn't care.

The man looked at him, then patted his chest hard.

"Szgany," he said, proudly.

Frye merely nodded and replied "Alexander."

The Szgany nodded back.

. . .

Hours passed and the cart, along with the day, trundled on. The journey had gone mostly in silence. The Szgany had shared some food and drink with Frye, for which he was grateful. He had not brought any of his own. Frye himself was about to try and ask how much further, when the Szgany suddenly pointed ahead.

"Dracula," he said, gesturing with emphasis.

Frye became instantly alert.

At first, he couldn't see anything, only the darkened branches of withered trees. Then they seemed to pull back like curtains, revealing the castle. Frye wanted to jump down from the cart and run towards it, but he calmed himself and allowed the Szgany to continue the journey. By the time they pulled into the courtyard, Frye felt like an excited child.

The cart came to a stop and Frye jumped down, looking up at the huge spires and towers with a sense of rapturous awe. Then his eyes fell upon another horse, saddled and tied up against an old tree. While he pondered this, the Szgany too jumped down from the cart and began walking toward the entrance, beckoning Frye to follow. Frye approached the doorway with him. To his surprise, the Szgany opened the door with ease, the hinges creaking like a bullfrog, before going inside. Frye followed.

The cold that greeted them was like a wall. Frye looked about him, as if he was in a holy place, there to worship his god. The castle entrance was a cavernous space, with solid stone pillars reaching high up to the ceiling, which in turn revealed old tattered flags hanging like bodies from the rafters. Across the great dark void, opposite the door, were great stone steps lined with fading tapestries, leading to other rooms and hallways. The stone walls held old torches, protruding at intervals around the vast space. The Szgany walked past the earth-box, glancing away from it as he did so. Frye saw it and gave a triumphant cry, running toward it and started pulling the loose lid away.

The Szgany witnessed what he was doing and ran over, shaking his head and trying to stop him, pleading *no* in a language Frye did not care to understand. Finally, the great wooden lid crashed to the floor, the sound echoing off the walls like an explosion. The Szgany turned away. Frye, on the other hand, looked in, seeing the ash. It had been protected, all this time. Dormant. Waiting for the spark of life.

Outside, darkness was beginning to fall.

The Szgany was in the full flow of his protestation when Frye caught hold of his head and thrust it hard against the side of the box. Staggering and confused, the Szgany did not know what was going on. Frye violently grabbed the man's head again and hit it against the box.

Frye did not want him dead, nor did he want him unconscious. The man was heavy, and Frye did not know if he could lift him. Instead, while the Szgany was insensible and controllable, he brought him to the side of the box and held his upper body over the rim.

Frye pulled a knife from inside his coat. He raised his face to the sky, as if basking in an invisible sun and said, "So you may be reborn."

He looked down at the Szgany and drew the sharpened blade across the man's throat. The gypsy man gave a yelp of pain and then a sickening gurgle as the warm, living blood spewed from the slice in his throat, all over the ash and dirt inside the earth-box. Frye held him there until the torrent became a drip before casting the body aside like a rag.

All was silent.

For a moment, Frye's faith faltered. Nothing was happening. He began to panic, thinking for an awful moment that his efforts had been in vain.

Then the old tattered flags began to move in an unseen breeze.

Suddenly he could feel it, creeping through the castle entrance and enveloping his body. It was soft at first, like a lover's caress, then it started building in intensity. The breeze became a howling wind, carrying fell voices that seemed to twist and creep around the stone walls and columns. Frye started smiling. This was it, the moment he had been waiting for. The herald of his master's return.

The wind gathered round the earth box and began to seep inside. Frye started to step closer, wanting to look, when a flash of lightning lit up the sky and thunder rumbled. Frye began to laugh at the glorious chaos, twirling his body round and round in ecstasy.

White, wispy smoke poured form the open box. It was like a witch's cauldron, brewing some strange spell. The wind caught it, and the smoke swayed like a snake. There were faces forming in the white tendrils – faces that looked like they were howling in pain and agony. Then a hand emerged from the milky soup, with pale, white skin, like marble. The long fingers gripped the edge of the box and started to pull, lifting the rest of the body out from the murk.

Silence fell once more. The kind of silence that felt like it covered the entire world. It was almost completely dark outside, and inside was now a domain of shadows.

Frye stopped twirling. He looked at the earth-box. Another hand emerged, then the body itself, the skin almost glowing in the gloom. It slithered out of the box like a slime covered slug, landing on the floor behind it. Frye was overcome with a rapturous joy.

"Master…" he whispered. He began approaching cautiously.

Suddenly, another sound pierced the silence. The sound of golden coins and precious jewels tinkling like glass as they tumbled down the stone stairs. Frye looked over toward the steps which led into the body of the castle. A man was standing there, holding a lit torch, whose flames were casting dark, dancing shapes behind him. He was carrying a sack which hung open in his hand, from which the valuable contents had spilled. On his face was a look of amazement and horror at the scene before him. Frye was unsure how much the man, who was dressed like his deceased former companion, had seen. Not that it would matter.

The Szgany dropped the sack of gold and

drew a sharp, vicious looking knife. He was speaking various curses and threats in his own language, none of which Frye could translate, though he understood the sentiment. Frye raised his own knife as the man came nearer.

With speed almost invisible to the eye, a white blur took the Szgany man off his feet and threw him into the blackness. His flaming torch fell to the floor, the fire flickering wildly. From the deep dark, Frye heard a brief yelp, then a growling, wrenching, tearing sound, like that of a dangerous predator, consuming its prey. Frye smiled. None of this held any fear for him, only triumph.

Suddenly, the torches on the walls flickered and flamed to life. Frye yelped with joy.

Standing there in the orange glow was a naked man. Thin like a wraith, with light grey hair covering his head. His ears were slightly pointed, as were his fingernails. His eyes blazed as red as the blood that ran down from his cruel mouth and onto his new-born flesh.

Frye immediately fell to his knees. "My lord Dracula, I am at your command."

He bowed low to the ground. Dracula smiled. He raised Frye up from the floor.

"You have done well, my faithful one" replied the Count. "When I called out to my followers at the time of my destruction, it was only you that answered."

Frye was in a state of rapturous pleasure at hearing that voice again.

"I live to serve you, my lord" Frye said. "All that I am is yours."

"Good. Then together, we will wreak my revenge upon the world."

Frye began to nod his head vigorously, the tears of joy at Dracula's return finally let loose. "Yes, Master," he cried. "Yes."

Chapter VI

19th November – London

Mina screamed and the relative peace of the last month was shattered.

Jonathan woke with a start. He had never heard such an utterance from his wife before – a noise like the fingernails of a thousand devils had pierced her flesh at once. When Jonathan looked toward his wife, she was, amazingly, still sleeping. Thrashing and bucking against the mattress, her eyes tightly shut, she was letting out piteous cries. He began to shake her awake.

"Mina!" he called. "Mina!"

Suddenly, the bedroom door burst open and

Van Helsing entered, pulling on his dressing gown. His red hair, now streaked with white, was ruffled, and his glasses sat askew on the edge of his nose. His appearance may have been comic if not for the circumstances. He had been staying with the Harker's since their return from Transylvania, keeping a close eye on Mina. She had made a miraculous recovery and the dreams had lessened in intensity. There were some nights she didn't dream at all. Now, it seemed, they had returned with a vengeance.

He went straight to Mina's side of the bed.

"Forgive me for the intrusion," he said to Jonathan apologetically. "But I thought I should…"

Jonathan waved the apology away. "Please. Help her."

The Professor laid a hand on her brow and pressed the other upon her stomach, gently but firmly pushing her body down upon the bed. He seemed to whisper soft but commanding words into her ear. Minutes passed. Slowly, the violent, jerky movements stopped.

"What happened to her?" asked Jonathan pleadingly.

"I do not know. A relapse of some kind."

"A relapse? My god, Professor! She was never like this, even before. I don't understand it."

Van Helsing tried to reply but realised he couldn't find the words. He was forced to admit he was at a loss.

Jonathan's eyes were fixed upon his wife. "I must see to Quincey. He must have heard. Please, take care of her."

Van Helsing nodded as Jonathan hurried from the room. When he got to Quincey's door, he found it already open. The maid, Christina, was sat on the bed in her nightgown. She was smoothing Quincey's hair down and speaking comforting words. She turned to toward the doorway, sensing Jonathan there.

"He's alright, sir. I've settled him."

"Thank you, Christina. Please, get yourself back to bed. I'll take over."

She stood. "Yes sir." She turned back toward Quincey. "Goodnight, young man." she said kindly.

"Goodnight," he replied, giving her a small wave.

She left the room.

Jonathan sat on the edge of the bed, stroking his son's cheek. "Are you alright?"

"Is Mother ill again?" Quincey asked, sadly.

"I don't know, son. I hope not. Uncle Abraham is looking after her."

Quincey gave a little nod and snuggled down further into his bedsheets.

"Try and go back to sleep, son." Harker leaned over his boy and kissed him on the forehead. "I love you."

"Love you too" he replied, already yawning.

Jonathan smiled sadly as he left the room and shut the door. He didn't know how much more any of them could take. He walked back to his bedroom with heavy footsteps.

When he got there, Mina was sat up in bed with a glass of water. Van Helsing had straightened up his appearance. He had pulled up one of the bedroom chairs and was sitting in it, listening to Mina's every word. Jonathan stood in the doorway, not wanting to interrupt.

Mina's voice was strained.

"It was like someone was squeezing my heart," she said. "Like they had actually reached into my chest and were holding it tightly, squeezing every bit of life from it."

"And who is it that was doing this thing?" asked the Professor, his voice calming. "Did you see a face?"

"Not a face, no. More like a… like a

shadow."

"When you think of that shadow, can you see any detail? Anything hidden in those depths?"

"Yes. One thing," replied Mina. "The same thing I always used to see in my dreams before, but clearer this time."

The Professor leaned forward. "And what is this one thing you saw, so clear?"

Jonathan stepped into the room now, though neither of them noticed his presence.

"Eyes," she said, her voice shaking. "Red eyes."

PART THREE

Chapter VII

22nd November – Aboard the Yasmin

The boat rocked gently back and forth. The sea had been kind, as had the weather. Alexander Frye walked along the deck through the many crewmen, all going about their duty. He was almost invisible to them, so little notice did they pay him. He had requested passage for himself and a single, large wooden box, no questions asked. The Captain had screwed up his face and offered lazy protestations, waiting for the inevitable offer of bribery, which came in the form of a large bag of gold.

When the Captain saw it, he did not haggle.

Frye had watched the box being loaded onto the *Yasmin* as if he were an expectant father. He admonished members of the crew for being rough with it, and demanded it was treated with more care. Once the box was in place, the crew had decided to ignore him completely for the remainder of the journey.

Frye visited the hold again. It was the fourth or fifth time that day. He checked the ropes holding down the box were secure and whispered the days progress to his Master as one would whisper a secret to a child. He walked back up on deck then, moving toward the bow and watching the land get ever closer. England. Oh, what glorious chaos would soon be wrought upon that land, he thought, smiling. Anything was possible now. His Master had retrieved much more gold and jewels from his treasures that the Szgany had not discovered. Frye knew of old that money could buy practically anything.

Dracula had fed heavily before boarding the ship. Once more, screams and cries of fathers and mothers were heard in the small villages of Transylvania, as they mourned the loss of their children.

The Count did not want to repeat the incident of the *Demeter,* the ship on which he had first travelled to England, and which arrived much like a ghost ship, with her dead captain lashed to the wheel. He knew that would alert his enemies to his return. It wasn't time for that.

Not yet.

But they would know soon enough.

23rd November – Creekmouth Port, London

It was early afternoon and tendrils of mist crept along the surface of the flat sea. The weather had been grey and miserable all day, and it didn't look like it was going to get any better.

The port was full of hustle and bustle, and the noise of orders and instructions being shouted from ship to shore, as cargo was being unloaded. Frye had been directed by the Captain on where to go to hire a horse, cart and driver. He was sat on the cart now, next to the rather craggy faced but jovial man who was driving it. Frye had been questioning the man about London, specifically areas that had empty buildings, like warehouses or factories. That was where he wanted to go. The Driver had looked curiously at him, not understanding his reasons. Frye had tried his best to convince him that he was looking for somewhere to re-develop.

The Driver simply nodded and shrugged his shoulders. He didn't believe any of it. Perhaps the box was full to the brim with stolen goods, he didn't care. He would let the little man spout his patently ridiculous excuses. He had been paid well and his pockets were heavy with golden coins.

The cart travelled along slowly. Frye noticed

how the streets had become grimmer and more desperate. There were not many people around, and those they did see looked dirty and unkempt. Then Frye noticed the old building. It had obviously been a factory of some kind but had not seen any business in many years. The building was fire damaged. He could see streaks of soot and burnt brick around the window frames. The rusted iron gates lay on the ground, bent and buckled like drunken men. Frye ordered the Driver to go through.

He pulled up his cart next to the entrance and Frye jumped down, walking through the door and into the vast, cavernous space. Whatever machinery had once been there was gone. The ground was covered in ash and dust and the whole space stunk of damp and desolation. It was perfect.

Outside, the Driver was becoming impatient. It was getting late, and he wanted to go home. He was about to shout out when Frye emerged from the dark doorway.

"Satisfied?" said the Driver, in a tone which suggested he didn't really care either way.

"Very" replied Frye, cheerfully.

"Well, you're going to need some help getting this box down from the cart. The two of us ain't going to manage it."

Frye smiled. "It won't be a problem" he said.

The last thing the Driver ever heard and smelt was the creaking of wood coming from behind him and an odour of death flowing over him like a wave.

23rd November

Mina began to whimper painfully in her sleep. She had started to dream of being trapped, as if her arms and legs were pinned down and unable to move. She was pressed in by something but couldn't work out what it was. Then she began to smell something. A mouldy, dank smell, like a garden after rain. That's when she realised – she was smelling dirt. She was trapped and surrounded by dirt, in a small, cramped space.

Then she began to cry out. The small space was the inside of a wooden earth-box. She started to wriggle and push against the compact soil, trying with all her might to free her arms. With a gargantuan effort, she was able to pull one arm free. She stretched out her fingers to feel the wooden lid above her. It was stuck fast. She pushed and pushed against it, finally freeing her other arm, which joined the efforts of the first. Pushing and pushing, but the lid would not move.

Then the earth inside the box began to rise like the water level of a river. Up and up, past her chin. She could taste the sour granules of dirt as they entered her mouth. It was starting to suffocate her. She tried to scream but couldn't.

And the level was getting higher.

Finally, she was able to let out a scream of agonising power, which reached out of her nightmare and into the real world. Jonathan had not yet gone to bed. He was downstairs, looking over some papers and documents for his work. The scream reached his ears in instant. He left the papers fluttering to the floor as he ran from his desk in the study. He bounded upstairs to his room, to see his wife struggling against the blankets covering her. He ripped them back and took hold of his wife's flailing arms. Jonathan held her close, protectively, calmly but firmly. He called her name softly until she woke.

Her body seemed to sag, and she peered at him through frightened tears before burying herself in his chest.

"Why won't this end?" she said desperately, her voice muffled by his shirt.

Jonathan didn't know what to say.

25th November

Jack Seward sat across from his wife at the dinner table. Stephanie was talking brightly about her day, laughing and smiling as she did so. Jack liked to watch her laugh. It made his heart glow and kept the memories of so very long ago at bay. There was never a day when the shadows of the past did not intrude upon him, as they did for all involved, but he felt so lucky to have this radiance in his life to make living worthwhile. She knew parts of it, of course, but not all. How anyone could relate the full story to another and not be treated much as he had to treat his own patients he did not know. But she always respected his wishes when it came to the past and welcomed his friends and companions warmly into their home, as they were welcomed into theirs. It was hard to pull away from these wonderful moments in order to attend to his work at the asylum, but reluctantly he gathered his things and kissed his wife warmly upon the lips. He had kept his private rooms at the asylum in case overnight work was required, as it was tonight.

A light rain was falling as he stepped into the waiting carriage, soaking the roads and pavements, and making the darkening world around him glow in the streetlight. During the carriage ride, he pondered Mina's dreams. He had been communicating back and forth with Van Helsing about them, trying in vain to find a solution.

When Jack got to the asylum he stared, as he always did, at the ruin of Carfax Abbey next door, another anchor to the past. As horrific as many of those memories were, he was also glad to have them, at times, as a symbol of friendship, strength and resilience.

He greeted the Attendants as always when he entered, not seeing Alexander Frye watching in the alleyway from the other side of the street.

Jack headed for his old rooms.

He entered and closed the door behind him. The room seemed colder than usual. And there was an unusual odour in the air. Like death. The smell brought back to him a hundred thoughts and feelings at once. His eyes widened in panic and a hundred puzzle pieces suddenly clicked into place. Hurrying to turn on the light, a swift bolt of cold air rushed past him and he felt a grip of iron around his throat. As his eyes began to adjust to the dark, a familiar aquiline face pierced the shadows, and deep inside that face glowed eyes of red.

"Welcome," spoke the familiar voice, with an air of self-satisfaction.

Jack struggled to answer, the grip around his throat was so tight. "But... How?" he gasped.

"How? How am I in these rooms or how have I returned?" Dracula replied, haughtily. "I will tell you. I have followers. Followers who I can bend to my will. Followers who would cross oceans to do my bidding. As for this room, well, an invitation once given, cannot be taken back." He smiled. "And my last visit here was oh, so sweet."

Jack's memory flashed back to the moment they found Dracula feeding on Mina, and forcing her to drink his own blood, binding them together and baptizing her with the vampire's curse.

"What are you going to do?" said Jack, still trying to pry his neck from the vampire's solid hold.

"Do? Why, win, of course. You and your friends won a battle, but the war is far from over. There are times a general must retreat and re-group, but always he will come back stronger."

Jack looked the vampire up and down. He did indeed look strong. Dressed in flowing black robes, his hair was iron grey and his jaw was set firm.

"Are you going to... turn me?" asked Jack, pleadingly. He immediately thought of his wife, and the danger she could be placed in.

"Turn you?" Dracula mocked. "No. Your ending will be much more final. You will die, Jack Seward. You are my message to them. You are an example of what lies ahead. They will not know where, they will not know when, they will know only, vengeance has come."

Before Jack could reply, Dracula tore his head off.

26th November – 5.00am

Inspector Ronald Wilton ran his eyes over the horrific scene again as he tried to piece together what had happened. Shaking his head at the level of carnage, he tried to remember another time in recent years when he had seen another murder as bad as this. He could not think of one. Wilton had been a young officer, newly appointed, when 'Jack the Ripper' stalked Whitechapel. He had not been heavily involved in that case, but he had seen the crime scene photographs and heard plenty of first-hand recollections. Even those horrific crimes would have a hard time matching up to the river of blood that had spread across the office floor of the deceased. He had met Seward many times during his duties and had liked him a great deal. How he could have met such a horrific end, Wilton could not imagine. The Attendants had discovered the apparent killer, a patient, wandering in Seward's private rooms, wading through the blood on his hands and knees, until he was slick with it. He was blabbering nonsense and seemed incredibly confused.

Wilton did not think he would get very far with questioning.

The patient was called Sanders. He was not a particularly large man, but the Attendants said he possessed prodigious strength. Whether he was strong enough to break the lock of his own room or, indeed, rip off a man's head was yet to be seen. There were no tools apparent – no knives, hammers or axes, that he could possibly have used.

The Inspector also knew his superiors would be happy with the neat bow presented to them – a crime committed and solved in one night, with the murderer already in custody and behind bars, that they would not be interested in any of his speculations. Wilton, however, did not believe in neat bows.

The next job was telling the widow.

Wilton was thankful the Attendants had identified Seward. That was an ordeal he did not want to put the poor man's wife through. He decided to reach out to Lord Godalming. He knew Seward and Godalming were old friends. The Inspector shared a mild acquaintance with Godalming himself – the Lord was an avid supporter of the police and they had both attended some of the same functions. Wilton thought that his presence when breaking the news to Mrs. Seward would perhaps soften the blow.

26th November

Later - Jonathan sat at the breakfast table, with Quincey on his knee. He was reading his son a story of knights and dragons, smiling as his son gasped and clapped excitedly at the clashing swords and fiery infernos.

He was extremely tired and doing his best to

hide it. Another bad night. Another frightening nightmare, but this time, no Van Helsing to ease his wife's mind. He had returned to Amsterdam to 'seek assistance' and would return shortly. Jonathan was worried. The last time such matters occurred, they were connected to Dracula, but the vampire was long gone. At least that's what Jonathan hoped. But with these recent incidents he had begun to feel a creeping dread, not felt since all those years ago in a castle in Transylvania.

Mina was fast asleep. He thought it best to let her rest. He didn't want anything to disturb her and hopefully, today, nothing would. He had left her there, sleeping, her hair spread out on the pillow like a halo.

He heard the front doorbell ring. Quincey didn't notice, he was too busy looking at the pictures in his book. Jonathan was sipping tea when Christina entered, holding an envelope.

"A telegram for you, sir," she said brightly.

"The young gentleman has been requested to take back an answer."

She handed him the envelope.

"Thank you, Christina," he said. He opened it and took out the telegram.

Raising his cup to his lips again, he began to read. It was from Arthur. Seconds later, the teacup tumbled to the floor and its contents spilled across the carpet.

"Jonathan?"

He looked up to see Mina in the doorway, pale and drawn from lack of sleep, a question in her eyes.

"What's happened?" she asked.

Quincey looked about, confused. Too much was happening at once.

"Christina, please take Quincey to his room" he said.

She acquiesced and took him out, quickly. Mina smiled at him as they passed. After they had left the room, she looked at Jonathan's face and her smile faded.

"What's happened?" she asked again.

"It's Jack," he said gravely. "He's dead."

1st December

Shafts of cold sunlight shone through the trees, and a calm breeze swept the remaining leaves from their branches. The friends were gathered again around the body of a brave companion. Arthur stood as if made of stone, his face as hard as granite. Beside him, his wife Laura comforted Stephanie, who was crying openly. Her grief had stolen her strength and so it was that both Laura and Mina held her tightly, in case she should happen to fall. Despite her own struggles, Mina stood resolute, with her husband by her side. Van Helsing had returned from Amsterdam. He too was stern in the face of this unspeakable tragedy. He had brought with him something of a surprise to all of them. A niece, Sophia. Twenty years old, as sprightly and as fiercely intelligent as her uncle. They were all shocked to find out that the Professor was her guardian. All his travels so many of those years ago, back and forth to Amsterdam, had been to ensure the safety and security of his niece. His sister was deathly ill at the time, so Van Helsing wanted to ensure that should anything happen to him or her, Sophia would be well looked after. He had not spoken to any of them of her existence for fear of her safety, should the Count have decided to focus his energies upon her. His sister had passed since then, and Sophia had come to live with him.

The minister finished his sermon and Jack's coffin was lowered into the ground. Stephanie began to wail. She reached out her hand pleadingly toward the coffin. She had been told that Jack was killed by an escaped inmate. One had been found out of his room; his door seemingly forced open somehow. His hands stained with Jack's blood.

None of them believed that story. Arthur especially, when listening to Inspector

Wilton relate the circumstances, could tell the Officer had little faith in the story he was telling.

Mina and Laura walked Stephanie reluctantly away from the graveside. Jonathan turned to leave. He motioned for Arthur to follow, but he shook his head. He wanted to remain longer. Jonathan nodded and walked away. Sophia and Van Helsing also departed, the Professor glancing back at his friends, and former pupils, resting place. Once the minster was gone, Arthur remained, alone.

He had been friends with both Quincey Morris and Jack for what seemed like forever, and now, to lose them both, was a hideous crushing blow. He gazed in at the earth-spattered coffin. He could have been there seconds, minutes or hours and not known.

"Bad way to go."

Arthur came out of his stupor and looked up to see a gravedigger leaning on his shovel, watching him.

"I beg your pardon?" said Arthur.

The gravedigger nodded toward the hole. "Bad way to go. Heard all about it."

Arthur supposed that gossip had gone around, even amongst the undertakers, but this man, this *stranger*, talking about the tragedy in such a way was nothing but impertinence.

"I'd rather not discuss it, thank you," replied Arthur, curtly. He began to turn away.

"Worse could be waiting" said the gravedigger.

Arthur snapped back. "What?"

Alexander Frye smiled. He had watched the whole funeral. The real gravedigger lay some feet away, unconscious or dead, Frye didn't care. Dracula had ordered him to 'stir the pot', and that is what he was doing.

"I said *worse could be waiting*, for you. And for your friends. His wrath is absolute." Frye smiled again.

Arthur became filled with a frightful rage. He began to run after the man. Frye dropped the shovel and sped away, with Arthur in pursuit. Spindly branches whipped them as they ran. Frye vaulted over gravestones, laughing. The cemetery gates were near. He was almost through them. Arthur stumbled on a protruding tree root but was up again in a moment. He started to run again, his fury giving strength to every stride. He made it to the gates and stepped out onto the street.

Arthurs piercing eyes as he scanned up and down the streets received odd looks from the people that were milling about. Carriages trundled by, and even an automobile, but no matter where he looked, his quarry was gone.

…

Later – The Tavern was smoky and full of chatter, which helped to cover the nature of their own conversation. Laura and Sophia had taken Stephanie home and had said they would stay with her a while.

The rest of them sat around a table, drinks ignored, while Arthur explained his encounter at the graveside. After he finished, they all sat silently, the realisation of everything he had told them washed over them like an icy wave. The Professor was the first to break the silence.

"So, I think we must all accept the fact, however unbelievable, that Dracula has returned."

"I don't understand, Professor," protested Arthur. "How can this be?"

"I do not know. In all the literature I have read, there has never been anything concerning resurrection of the un-dead."

He didn't mention, at that juncture, the part he thought Mina's dreams were playing in all of this.

As they sat thinking, Sophia joined them at the table.

"Stephanie is sleeping," she said. "Laura said she would stay with her a while. I thought I should come back."

Sophia knew every part of the history concerning the circle of friends. A student of the occult, much like her uncle, Van Helsing swore she would play a valuable part in whatever lay ahead. They had all welcomed her immediately.

"Will she be safe?" asked Arthur. "At the house, I mean."

"I think so," replied the Professor. "I find it very telling that Dracula should murder Jack at the asylum and not at his home."

Jonathan queried.

"Remember," interjected Sophia, "a vampire cannot enter a residence without permission. He already had permission to enter the asylum."

Jonathan nodded.

"And he doesn't actually know where any of

you live."

They all nodded at that, giving as it did a small measure of comfort.

The first thing they all decided to do from there was arm themselves, as they did of old, with a crucifix. He may not know, as Sophia said, where any of them live, but that didn't mean he wouldn't try to find out. This man, Frye, was clearly dangerous and unpredictable and Dracula could obviously use him any way he saw fit. To that end, they would each add to their personal defences a revolver.

"We must be vigilant," concluded Van Helsing "and check newspapers every day for any strange story that may help us determine where Dracula is hiding. He is here to destroy us, yes, but we will destroy him first."

Chapter VIII

8th December

A week had passed and no further attempts on their lives had been made.

They scanned the newspapers religiously, but no reports could be found of anything unusual. When Lucy had been turned, the papers had referred to her as the 'bloofer lady', which was a nickname given to her by the small children she prayed on. But there were no 'bloofer ladies', no mutilated bodies. Van Helsing determined that Dracula may be feeding on the homeless to try and hide his whereabouts. And that he was deliberately letting time pass, in order to keep them all on edge.

And through it all, Mina's dreams were getting worse.

Images of death and hatred, planted in her head like a malignant seed, were sprouting like a rotten tree. She stayed in her bedroom most of the day, trying to catch up on stolen sleep, barely eating. Jonathan, Van Helsing and Sophia took turns in watching and caring for her, as well as comforting Quincey and keeping him occupied. No matter what they did, nothing could seem to ease her suffering.

After eight hours of bedside vigil, Van Helsing sat in the study, leaning forward in his chair, head in his hands. He had come to several conclusions in the last few days and none of them gave him any comfort. Jonathan entered and Van Helsing looked up, questioningly.

"Quincey is sleeping. And Sophia is watching Mina" said Jonathan in answer. "She is a remarkable young woman."

Van Helsing smiled as Jonathan sat next to him. "Indeed, she is. I cannot say her mother was happy when little Sophia began to take interest in her mad uncle's schemes and ideas so young, but she came to get used to it."

"I'm glad for that," sighed Jonathan. "We're going to need all the help we can get. I cannot help thinking about poor Jack, what happened to him. After everything we went through…"

"He was the best student I ever had. And one of my best friends." The Professor suddenly shook his head brusquely. "No, he was my family."

"Yes. I thought of him like a brother. Like I think of you and Arthur."

They sat silently for a while, unspoken questions passing between them. The air seemed alive with them. Finally, Jonathan broke the silence. To Van Helsing, it was like a storm breaking.

"Professor, what is wrong with Mina?"

Van Helsing sighed and leaned far back in his chair. "The answer to this question I have been pondering for some time. I have read many books and made many assumptions, but I believe I have an answer. But Jonathan, my boy, this answer may be hard for you to hear."

"It doesn't matter. I have to hear it."

"Yes," Van Helsing relented. "You do."

Before he spoke, he stood and walked to the sideboard, pouring two glasses of whisky. He handed one to Jonathan before sitting back down.

"Dracula and Mina, after everything that happened before, are linked. And will be linked for all time."

A look of disbelief crossed Jonathan's face. "But how can that be? When he was destroyed the curse passed away..."

Van Helsing sipped his whisky. "That is

true. But his blood had run completely through her veins, you see? They were one. Connected. And when he was destroyed, it is true, his ability to have control over her was gone, but he was close, so close, to controlling her forever."

Jonathan took a drink before hanging his head.

"I believe" the Professor continued, "that Mina's dreams were a manifestation of Dracula's soul calling to her from hell itself."

Jonathan stood up straight, like a rod of iron. "That's not possible."

"Oh, my boy, in this world of vampires and evils of the night, all is possible. She is like an anchor for him."

Jonathan sat back down slowly. He took another drink.

"That so awful dream Mina had, in November," Van Helsing continued, "when she scream so terribly. When she talk of red

eyes and dark visions becoming clear. I
believe that was the very night Dracula
returned to this earth. And then again, the
night of Jack's horrible death. Yes, she is
connected to him and he is to her."

"Do you mean to tell me," said Jonathan
"that even if we destroy him again, Mina
will…"

"She will go back to how she was before.
She will dream of his soul in hell."

Jonathan finished his drink. "Maybe it won't
be as bad. As before."

"I… I cannot really say," said the Professor.
Even as those words passed his lips, Van
Helsing knew it was nothing but an empty
hope, anything to give Jonathan some
strength.

Silence descended between them again.

Suddenly, the study door creaked open.
They both looked, expecting to see
Quincey's mischievous face peering through
the gap. Instead they saw Mina. Gaunt and

pale but resolute. Sophia stood behind her.

"Mina…" Jonathan rushed forward and helped his wife to a chair. "You need to rest."

"I couldn't stop her" said Sophia apologetically.

Mina took hold of the arms of the chair to give herself some support. Sophia stood behind her, like a guard.

"I want you to do something for me, Abraham," said Mina. Her voice was strong, but they could detect a slight tremor in it, the only thing that betrayed her weakened state. And they all noted her use of the Professor's first name. "I want you to hypnotise me, as you used to do. It is obvious to me that the connection he… Dracula and I… had before is still there. Maybe if you hypnotise me, we can find where he is. And maybe then… well, we can bring this thing to an end."

Jonathan felt such a sense of pride in that moment. Despite everything, once again,

Mina was able to say all that needed to be said.

"I had been thinking the same," replied Van Helsing. "But in your delicate condition, I was afraid to ask."

"It must be done," she said. "It's time our fear was his."

Jonathan bowed his head and Sophia placed a comforting hand on Mina's shoulder.

Van Helsing stood and addressed them all.

"Tomorrow then, at dawn."

9th December

The sky was a deep purple, with a few twinkling stars remaining, when Van Helsing and Sophia entered Mina and Jonathan's room. Dawn was approaching. Mina was awake and ready, propped up on her pillows. Jonathan stood by her, on ever-present watch. The Professor held a lit candle, which he bade her watch, her eyes following the flame as he passed it slow from side to side, in front of her face. His voice was quiet, but deep and commanding, leading her into a hypnotic trance. Sophia watched closely, fascinated at a sight which she had heard of, but never seen.

Finally, Mina's eyes closed. The Professor put the candle down on the bedside table and began to speak.

"Where are you?"

"It is dark. Some kind of cellar. Or large room. The walls are made of brick." Her voice was soft but clear.

"What do you hear?"

"Nothing. It is very quiet here."

Van Helsing decided to be more direct. "Where is your earth-box?" he asked.

"It is here. It is hidden from the likes of you."

They all stole glances at each-other, then stared at Mina. Her voice had become momentarily mocking and arrogant.

"Are you near the centre of the city?" he continued.

Suddenly, Mina began to laugh, but it was not her laugh at all. It was harsh and cruel. "Ask your questions, you old fool, but you will receive no answers from me."

Jonathan panicked. "Break the link, Professor, quickly!"

Instead, Van Helsing persevered, determined not to be bettered by the Count.

"You have found a way to communicate through Mina."

"All those years in hell, I have thought of nothing else but this. I have marshalled all the forces of darkness within me in order to guarantee my victory." Mina's face seemed to change. It became stern and cruel.

"You will find no victory here," said the Professor.

Mina laughed again. "Did I not tell you, all those years ago, that I commanded nations, hundreds of years before you were born? Pit your wits against me this time and I guarantee you will fail. I am not here to conquer. This time, I am here to destroy."

Suddenly, her eyes flicked open, and there, in the pupils, blazed a red light. Laughing, she looked about the entire room, fixing her gaze upon them one by one, before the light flickered and faded, her body convulsed, and Jonathan rushed to grab her before she fell out of bed onto the floor.

9th December – cont'd

Alexander Frye had been stood outside the Traveller's Rest tavern for what seemed like an age. The streetlights were lit and bathed everything in a golden glow. He had been watching and waiting patiently, eyeing each person as they left, gauging their level of inebriety. Finally, a man exited the tavern who seemed right for his purpose. The man staggered and almost fell, and his sense of direction seemed confused.

Frye approached and offered kind

assistance. He spoke helpful and encouraging words, which the man responded too. He smelled strongly of whisky and Frye chuckled that the drunkard's breath alone could easily have intoxicated a sober man.

Frye half led, half carried the man toward a quieter, more ruinous part of the city, full of empty, dilapidated warehouses and residential properties. One of the buildings was an old paper-mill, burnt down some years ago. The place Frye had chosen for his Master. It was mostly a darkened shell, the ground covered in dirt and piles of sodden ash. Waiting in the darkened entrance way was Dracula, his black cloak floating on a strong breeze.

The drunk man, perhaps sobered by the cold air, suddenly realised he was not going in the direction he needed to go. He began to pull, feebly, against Frye's grip, but he was not strong enough to break it. Then he saw Dracula, standing, smiling, like a ravenous cat stares at a mouse. The man began to pull harder, then whimper and call out. With an unseen movement, Dracula grabbed the man by the throat and pulled him into the darkness. He screamed once, the sound echoing off the stone walls, and was then silent forevermore.

Frye entered the old structure. The drunk man's body had been cast aside and already forgotten. Frye noticed the man's head was bent at an odd angle – broken, to prevent any chance of turning. Dracula stood, imperious and menacing in the gloom. Shafts of moonlight shone through the glassless windows.

"Tonight, my vengeance goes one step further. That fool Van Helsing has allowed me to regain my connection to Mina. I know now where they are."

"Will we kill them all, my Lord?" asked Frye.

Dracula turned to face him. Frye bowed his head.

"No, not yet," he said, smiling. His pointed white teeth glinting in the white light. "We have cut off one arm. Tonight, we will cut off another. We will take them slowly, piece by piece."

Frye smiled, looking back up at his Master with fanatical glee. "Yes, my Lord."

Chapter IX

9ᵗʰ December – cont'd

Arthur had joined his friends at Harker's house. His wife, as understanding as ever, had let him go reluctantly and with much sorrow. She could see pain in his eyes as he left her. A sign of a man slowly breaking under pressure. They had stayed with Stephanie a while, and all that time Laura could see her husband not only living with this new grief over losing Jack but re-living his loss of Quincey Morris all over again.

He sat now outside Mina's room, a revolver and a crucifix within arm's reach. There were droplets of sweat upon his brow.

Little Quincey was fast asleep. The adults

had made such a fuss over him and tired him out completely. He had sensed tension amongst them, but during hours of games and stories it was mostly forgotten.

Jonathan, Sophia and Professor Van Helsing sat in the study, all of them armed like Arthur, but Jonathan had added his kukri knife to his arsenal. The same knife which had slit the vampire's throat so long ago. Van Helsing had prepared wooden stakes. Three of them, all of which were lined up on the table like soldiers. Sophia held her crucifix in her hand, twirling it absent-mindedly round and round in her fingers.

They were all silent, loaded with the expectation that *something* was going to happen tonight.

...

In the kitchen, Christina washed the dinner-plates. Most of the food was wasted, as no one seemed to want to eat anything. There was a strange mood in the house. An electricity in the air. She shook off the unpleasant feeling.

Suddenly, there was a knock at the backdoor. She jumped slightly at the sound. Turning to look, she saw her fiancé's face smiling at her through the glass.

"Tommy!" she said excitedly, as she wiped the dishwater off her hands and opened the door.

"Alright, beautiful?" His smile was full of joy as he took her in his arms, kissing her on the lips.

Christina giggled, then turned to look behind her, in case anyone in the house had heard. She looked back. "I wasn't expecting you tonight."

"I know. I thought I'd surprise you." He kissed her again. "Do you wanna go for a turn around the park before bedtime?"

She pursed her lips into a slight pout. "I can't now. I've got all this cleaning up to do." She gestured at all the plates. "Cook's already gone home. I'm on my own."

"No worries, little dove," he said brightly. "I'll come back. Half an hour?"

"Won't that be too late?"

"Of course not! You'll be with me. Safe as houses."

She agreed readily and kissed him again as he left. She closed the door and waved through the window at him as he wandered off into the dark. Christina turned back to her work and started again. She was positively sprightly now, knowing Tommy would be coming back for her. A few moments more passed in blissful ignorance when another knock came at the door. Confused that Tommy had come back so much sooner than expected, she didn't even look as she opened the door. His name was about to escape her lips when Alexander Frye slipped like an eel through the door, firmly grasping a hand around her mouth and wrapping his arm around her body, pinning her arms to her sides.

"Don't move, don't speak, don't scream," he

ordered, the words hissing like acid in her ear. He turned her violently toward the open back door. Where she saw Tommy. He too had his mouth covered, but by a hand with long white fingers and sharpened nails. Her eyes hovered upward to the man standing behind her fiancé. He had a cruel face and piercing, unforgiving eyes.

"That is my Master" said Frye. "He wishes to come in. You will invite him."

Christina tried to turn her head toward Frye, her eyes pleading. He shook his head.

"No, no," he uttered impatiently. "No questions now. It's very simple. You will say the words 'come in', or your lover there will die before your eyes." Frye took his knife from his coat and brandished the blade before her face. Her body tensed in his grip. She looked back out at Tommy, his eyes wide with panic. Dracula raised his free hand and lightly let his sharp fingernail run down the side of Tommy's face, leaving a trail of blood in its wake. He winced.

"I'm going to uncover your mouth now," continued Frye, calmly. "If you scream, he dies."

Frye peeled his fingers away from her mouth. "Now, invite my Master in."

Christina's eyes searched all around her for a way out. She knew if she invited this *thing* into the house, for it was no ordinary man, great harm would follow. She looked out again at her fiancé. Dracula was tightening his grip around Tommy's face. His skin was turning red.

"Do it!" Frye ordered. "This is the last time I will ask."

Christina closed her eyes and whispered under her breath. "God forgive me." She opened them and looked squarely at the sinister man. "Come in," she said.

Then, many things happened at once. Dracula smiled. Frye plunged his knife into Christina's back, while covering her mouth again, in case she should scream. As the blood left her body and her eyes began to droop, the last thing she saw was Tommy, struggling to scream beneath Dracula's grip, before the vampire broke his neck, as easy as snapping a twig. They let the bodies slump to the floor.

Upstairs in her bedroom, Mina screamed.

The whole house was instantly alerted.

Frye entered the main body of the house. He was in the hallway, with doors on his left and right. He also saw the stairs, which is where he wanted to go. He began to creep forward, when a door on his left swung open and Jonathan Harker appeared. Frye ducked into the alcove beneath the stairs.

"Is everything alright?" Jonathan called up.

"I think so. It must just be another dream."

Frye recognised that voice. It was Arthur. He remembered it from Seward's funeral. Another person appeared then. A girl. He had seen her with the others but was unsure of who she was. He saw her put a reassuring hand on Harker's arm.

"I will go up and check on her. And Quincey," she said. "You stay here."

"Thank you, Sophia," replied Harker, as the girl walked up the stairs.

Harker returned to the room on his left.

Frye emerged from the alcove and began a slow, creeping ascent upstairs.

. . .

In the study, Jonathan paced back and forth. Van Helsing watched him with concern in his eyes.

"You must be calm," said the Professor. "Dracula cannot enter. We will be ready for whatever he tries."

"I know this. I know, but it was all so different before," he exclaimed.

"How different?"

"We knew where he was. We had a plan.

We had strategy. Sitting and waiting… it's driving me mad." Jonathan slumped into a chair.

"Better that we sit and wait than go out into the night, leaving Mina and Quincey unprotected."

Jonathan looked at the Professor. As always, his calming logic had the desired effect. He sat back in his chair and sighed, resigning himself to waiting.

…

Frye reached the top of the stairs. The landing curved to the right so he could not see the upstairs layout, or where Arthur and the girl, Sophia, were going to be. He crouched down on the last few steps and peered around the corner. At the very end of the landing, he could see Arthur, sat on a chair outside what he assumed was Mina Harker's bedroom. He had a revolver in his hand.

Sophia came out of a door on the right,

closing it behind her.

"Is he alright?" asked Arthur.

"He's awake," she replied. "And restless. He's worried about his mother."

"Of course."

"I'll just go in and see her."

Arthur stepped aside and let Sophia enter Mina's bedroom. Arthur stood facing the bedroom door. He put the revolver down on his seat.

Frye continued to watch.

Suddenly, a young child came out of the room on his right. A boy.

Frye's eyes widened. The child was only a few feet away.

"How is Mama?" asked the child.

Arthur began to turn toward the tiny voice as Frye sprung from his hiding place.

...

In the study, both Jonathan and Van Helsing began to feel tired. Distracted somehow. The room suddenly felt close, like it was contracting around them. There seemed to be specks in the air, floating in front of their faces, making circles and shapes. It was with a sudden sense of dawning horror that they both realised they were being hypnotised. But the realisation came too late. A creeping mist entered the room. It swept across the floor, probing the corners of the study with wispy fingers. Then it seemed to form into a pillar. And out of the pillar stepped a man. A man they both knew. The mist dissipated and only Dracula remained. He smiled at them both, helpless and pinned to their chairs.

"Gentlemen," he said, his voice low and commanding. "A pleasure to see you both once again, after all this time."

He turned his gaze specifically toward Jonathan. "And how is your wife?"

Dracula laughed as Jonathan tried to regain

control of his body.

"I'm… going to… kill you." Jonathan said, finally.

Dracula looked pityingly at him. "I think we both know by now death is not as final as we would hope it to be. But it matters not. Something much worse waits for you." He turned to Van Helsing then. "For you all."

The door to the study opened then and Arthur, Sophia and Mina entered. They all looked lost and defeated. Mina stood only with Sophia's help. Arthur kept mouthing *sorry*, over and over. Finally, Alexander Frye entered the room. He had Arthurs revolver pressed against Quincey's head.

"I'm so sorry, Jonathan, Mina." Arthur fell to his knees. "He grabbed Quincey. Put a knife to his throat… please forgive me."

"Shut up!" commanded Frye.

Quincey was crying. Mina tried to reach for him.

"Don't touch him!" Frye ordered. "Or he dies."

Mina looked helplessly on at the scene before her. "It will be alright, my love," she said to Quincey, her words catching in her throat. "It will be alright."

Quincey's crying started to subside into a whimper.

Dracula looked at the boy. He knelt and stared into Quincey's face. "Handsome boy," he said, looking at Mina. "He has your eyes." He stood again and surveyed the room.

"Should any of you try to use a crucifix against me, the boy will die. Understand?" He took their silence as agreement. "I want you all to know, that this will not be the end of your torment. What happens here tonight will crush your spirits so, that you will not even want to carry on. But you will have to. The choice will not be yours, but mine."

As Dracula spoke, Van Helsing began to

shake off the vampire's influence. His own strong will fought back, and he found that he could move again. As quick as he could manage, the Professor grabbed a single wooden stake from the table and lunged at Dracula. Sophia shouted out in horror as the vampire deftly grabbed Van Helsing's wrist, turning it and twisting it until the old man could do nothing but fall to his knees.

"Your will was always strong, Van Helsing," hissed the vampire. "But your flesh is weak."

Dracula casually took the stake from the Professor's hand. He looked at it a moment, this thing that had been made specially to bring about his destruction. He brought the wooden point down toward Van Helsing's chest, letting it rest over his heart.

Mina began to weep. Sophia made as if to move forward, when a warning look from Frye stopped her. Arthur could barely look, while Jonathan continued to struggle against Dracula's influence.

Van Helsing looked at each of them in turn, his eyes resting on Sophia. He smiled at her. "Don't be afraid," he said softly.

With that, Dracula punctured his heart with the stake, using all his might to thrust the weapon completely into the Professor's chest. Sophia screamed as the light left her dear uncle's eyes. Dracula let his body fall to the floor. All that intelligence, intellect and love, extinguished.

With a scream of rage, Jonathan finally broke Dracula's mental hold over him. He leapt up from his seat, scrambling to reach his kukri knife. Dracula slapped him away, as if he were an insect. Jonathan flew back into the bookcase and onto the floor, groaning in pain. Quincey had started to cry again, his tears flowing freely, his wailing sobs filling the air.

The Count turned toward Mina, his red eyes blazing in triumph. "You were going to be my bride once, but you turned away from an immortal life and chose to aid these insects against me. So now, perhaps, instead of a bride, I will have a son."

Mina yelled in horror as Dracula nodded toward his minion, and Frye, as quickly and quietly as a snake, took tight hold of Quincey and ran from the house into the night. Mina tried to follow, her desperation fuelling her strength, but Sophia pulled her back.

"Don't!" she cried. "It will do no good."

Mina broke free of Sophia's grip and fell at Dracula's feet. She took hold of his cloak, pulling it and tugging it in agonising fury.

"Take me!" she screamed, over and over.

"Tomorrow," he said, revelling in her misery. "Hyde Park. Noon."

In the blink of an eye, the cloak, the man, was gone and a swarm of large grey rats seemed to cover the study floor like a blanket. They crawled over the furniture, over their feet, over Jonathan and over Van Helsing's lifeless body. Mina covered her ears against their sickening squeals as the rats poured out of the room and into the hallway. Sophia followed them as they squirmed into the kitchen. She slammed open the kitchen door, revealing Christina and her fiancé, lying prostrate, both with the unmistakable look of death.

The last rat escaped through the back door as she got there. Expecting to see the rustling forms escaping into the alleyways, she instead saw a large bat, flying away in the moonlight.

But the night was far from over.

PART FOUR

Chapter X

10th December – 1am

Jonathan walked as if in a daze, surveying the carnage of the last hour. Blood and tragedy and death seemed to fill every corner of his home.

He peered into his son's room; its very emptiness made his whole world feel meaningless. As each incident played over and over in his head, it seemed as if a fist was being pummelled into his gut. He heard a shuffling footstep behind him and turned to see Arthur. He was deathly pale, and lines of exhaustion had seemingly been drawn upon his face.

"I am so sorry, Jonathan."

"Sorry?" he replied. "What for? You did all you could."

Arthur shook his head, feebly. "No. I didn't… I couldn't do… anything. It's like my courage has gone. It's deserted me. And now, Van Helsing and your poor son…" He collapsed onto the floor.

Jonathan knelt beside him. "It's alright, Arthur. You can't blame yourself. You can't. How could we ever have known that it would come to this?"

Arthur turned away from Jonathan's gaze. "I can't do this anymore."

"What do you mean?"

"I mean, I can't fight. Not anymore. I'll gladly take you into my house. I'll clothe you, feed you, anything you need, but I can't fight. I can't."

Jonathan nodded. He knew that Arthur had come to the end of this road. As devastated as he was, he understood. And he also knew the help Arthur had just offered would be necessary with what came next.

…

The house burned, a beacon of sorrow in the shadows of the night. Jonathan had a face set in stone as he poured oil on the furniture and floor, setting matches to crumpled paper and watching the flames take flight.

They knew they could never return to that place of death and darkness, and that they could not hope to explain to any authorities about what had happened within those walls. Better an 'accidental' fire covers the horrors within. Jonathan and Mina, with bundles of their belongings beneath their arms, could only afford mere seconds of contemplation, watching their home dissolve in the angry flames.

The sound of fire alarm bells ringing in the distance carried them away into the night.

Arthur turned back to look for just a moment, before turning away again, tears burning his face, as hot as the inferno behind him. Sophia continued to stare at the fire, which had become a funeral pyre for her Uncle. She hoped the flames would carry his brave spirit to heaven.

...

The carriage ride happened in silence, each of them processing their feelings of shock and grief. It was more than an hour before they got to Arthur's home. Here Arthur and Laura were Lord and Lady Godalming. The servants were roused, and rooms quickly prepared for their new guests. Laura had questions for each of them, but knew now was not the time, she merely welcomed them warmly and made sure all of them were comfortable. Jonathan and Mina lay in bed, holding each-other tightly. Sophia sat in solitude. She had hurriedly grabbed her uncle's crucifix before leaving. She sat with it now, staring at herself in the reflective silver.

Downstairs in the drawing room, the fireplace was lit. Arthur could not bear to look at the flames. Laura sat next to him, her hands clasping his. He had told her about the fire, but no more than that.

"Arthur, I have never asked you to explain what happened to you and your friends all those years ago. I can't say I was happy about it, but I respected it. It was clear you all shared a bond and I never wanted to get in the way of that."

"You never have, Laura, I promise you."

She stroked his hair. "But you are a changed man, my love. You are broken. I've watched you these last weeks, slowly crumble before my eyes. Please, tell me what is going on."

He looked up at her, his eyes wet and glistening. "Not for all the money in the world would I tell you of such horrors. You mustn't ask me."

"But Arthur, where is Quincey? Has he been kidnapped? Has he been sent away? What is happening? My god, he's just a small boy!"

He stood and walked toward the fireplace, leaning on the mantle. "I wouldn't even know where to start."

"Shouldn't we call the authorities?"

He shook his head. "It would do no good."

"But how?" she pleaded. "Why?"

He turned toward her. "You wouldn't understand. No one would. But he'll be safe, somehow. Jonathan, Mina, Sophia, they'll get him back."

She looked on him with pained eyes, confused and unsure. "Are you going to help them?" she asked.

"I can't!" he exclaimed. "I can't. I cannot help them anymore."

Laura stood and walked slowly over to him. "I can't lie Arthur; I'm relieved that you've decided to walk away from this madness. But are you? Can you live with that decision?"

He couldn't answer in words. He looked at his wife, tears streaming down his face. She opened her arms for him, and he buried his grief in her welcoming embrace.

10ᵗʰ December – 11.30am

The sun in the park was shining, but the light was cold. There were only a few people strolling in the park, put off perhaps, by the cold weather. Flashes of sun-dappled breath escaped from their mouths as they walked along. Jonathan and Mina sat on a bench. The autumn air all around them seemed to stab at their skin. Sophia had been in the park the longest, doing her best to stay hidden, searching for any sign of Frye. They also had a carriage at the park entrance, ready for them at a moment's notice.

The last twenty-four hours had taken a very heavy toll, and despite whispers of comfort and encouragement, nothing could bring them out of the sea of melancholy in which they all seemed to be drowning. The parting at Arthur's home that morning was strained and uncomfortable for all of them, an uneasy mixture of understanding and a desperate hope that he would choose to join them once again. Arthur could only apologise once more and promise that his home would remain theirs until all of this was over.

Jonathan came back to the present when Mina nudged him slightly with her elbow. He looked up to see Frye walking towards them. They both stood, attempting a show of strength against the sickening smile spread across the man's smug face.

"Pleasure to see you both again," said Frye. "I realised, during all of last night's excitement, that I never introduced myself." He offered a mocking nod of greeting. "Alexander Frye."

"Where are you keeping our son?" asked Jonathan, sternly.

Frye laughed. "Oh, what a bundle of energy he is! Quite a handful." He began to look about him, as if he was distracted. "He's safe."

Mina took a compulsive step forward. "Give him back!"

Frye focused his gaze on her. "My Master says you can have him back, but you must give something to him in return."

"What does he want?" said Mina, impatiently, sick of the ridiculous dance.

Frye smiled again, still focusing himself upon her. "Why, *you*, of course."

Jonathan's anger flared. "What?!"

Frye's gaze shifted to Jonathan. "Seven years ago," he said "my Master claimed your wife as his own. She was taken away. He wants her back. His castle is very lonely now his brides have been so cruelly murdered. He needs another."

"No dammit!" exclaimed Jonathan.

Mina held his arm, trying to calm the violence of his response. They were beginning to draw unwelcome looks from the public.

"He can't have her," Jonathan continued, venomously.

Frye did not seem unduly perturbed. "If Mina agrees to join my Master, you can have your son back. If not... well, you may have to live the rest of your lives knowing he now calls Dracula *father*."

Jonathan sank back down onto the bench. Mina sat beside him, taking his hand.

"We knew to expect something like this," she said, gently.

"I can't lose you" he replied.

"You can't lose me. I'm here." She pressed her hand over his heart.

He bowed his head, resigned to whatever fate had in store. Mina stood again and looked directly at Frye. Her demeanour was calm and her voice steady.

"What must I do to get our son back?"

"At nine pm tomorrow evening, you will arrive at St. Katherine's Dock. There is a ship there called the *Groza*. No crew will be aboard. They have all been paid well enough to leave the ship empty until we set sail the following morning. The two of you will go aboard, where my Master will be waiting. As will I. Once you are there, your son will be returned to you. And you…" he looked at Mina, "will willingly join my Master." He gave a sudden flourish with his hands. "And all will be well."

He bowed to them both before turning and walking away.

About twenty yards away, well hidden by trees and foliage, Sophia watched, with anger burning within her chest. She paid close attention to the direction Frye was taking. He obviously expected to be followed, so was taking a deliberately circuitous route out of the park, which eventually led to him going over his own tracks. Her heart skipped with victorious expectation when she saw him exit the park very near to where her carriage was waiting. Following carefully, Sophia saw Frye jump aboard a large cart, with room enough on the back, she noticed, for a large box. She allowed him to pull away before stepping aboard her own carriage and instructing the driver to follow with as much caution as he could muster.

Frye was in no undue hurry and so the journey progressed at a maudlin pace. Sophia made sure to note the streets and alleyways, all the points of reference that she could possibly remember. The hustle and bustle around the park and the inner parts of London began to lessen somewhat as they approached what Sophia assumed was their destination. A burnt-out factory, with windows that looked like hollowed out eyes. The cart ambled through the open gates and toward the main entrance. Frye stopped the cart and got down, entering the building.

So, this was it then. The Counts resting place. Quincey's prison.

She would have to get back to Jonathan and

Mina as quickly as possible. Plans needed to be made and their own vengeance served.

Chapter XI

10th December – 3.30pm

Sophia sat with Jonathan and Mina in the
bedroom gifted to them by Arthur and
Laura. They felt it best to speak and plan in
private. Arthur still felt a crippling shame
for pulling out of the fight and could not
easily look any of them in the eye, despite
all their kind words of understanding and
patience. He continued to offer anything else
they might need, including any hunting
equipment, like knives and rifles. Sophia
chose to dress as if she *were* a hunter,
including trousers instead of skirts, for ease
of movement. She also borrowed one of
Arthurs hunting knives, which had a

wickedly sharp blade.

They decided to head to the burnt-out factory that evening. Autumn nights had already made the sky dark and grey, so sunlight was not a factor. Dracula would be there, and he would be able to use all his strength against them. They just had to be ready. Jonathan had his kukri knife and they all carried a crucifix. Sophia had suggested revolvers, but Mina quickly objected. Quincey would be in enough danger without stray bullets flying.

There were no other access points to the paper-mill that Sophia had seen, so their only option was the front entrance.

Before venturing out, they stood in a circle and prayed quietly together.

Suddenly, the front doorbell rang.

They all looked at each-other, their faces enveloped in sudden panic. Some minutes ticked by. They stayed completely quiet, unsure of what was going on below them.

There was a quiet knock at the bedroom door and Laura entered. She gestured for them to be quiet.

"There is a Police Inspector downstairs," she whispered. "Talking to Arthur. It's about the fire."

…

Inspector Wilton looked at the haggard complexion on Lord Godalming's face and saw tragedy etched there. He regretted having to come, but there was once again some strange connection between a serious incident and with Lord Godalming. The home of Jonathan Harker, a Solicitor and friend to the Lord, burnt down. Bodies inside. Three of them. None of them readily identifiable. No idea if it was the Harker family or not.

He had found Godalming's reaction odd. A kind of pained look had come across his face, and an exclamation of shock, but there was a ring of detachment about it. He decided, finally, to be more forward in his questioning. The two men sat opposite each other, as if they were in an interview room.

"Lord Godalming," he began, "please forgive my impertinence, but I have to ask you something."

"Please, go ahead" replied Arthur.

"Do you know something about what's going on here? It's just, I can't help but notice, you have had a close personal connection with the victims of two serious crimes..."

"So, you think it is a crime then?" interrupted Arthur. "And not an accident?"

"Well, all the evidence isn't in yet, but I'd safely put a bet on it, yes sir" said Wilton gravely.

"I see. So, what is it you want to say?"

"Are you in danger of some kind? Are you being targeted in some way? You and your friends?"

Arthur wanted to blurt it all out then and

there but feared he would be called a madman. However, he saw an opportunity to plant a seed that may bear fruit at some later point.

"There is something I need to tell you. I don't know if it will help but I think it needs mentioning."

The Inspector leaned forward. "Go ahead, sir" he said.

"There was a man," began Arthur. "At Jack's funeral. I thought, at first, he was a gravedigger. I was alone at the graveside. This man, he began to make… comments."

"What kind of comments?"

"Unpleasant comments. Like threats. Saying that awful things were going to happen to my family and friends. Just as bad as what happened to Jack."

"I see" said the Inspector. "And why didn't you come to us about this man?"

Arthur decided to tell him the truth about his

first impressions of Frye. That he was indeed, just being impertinent and overtly threatening. He declined to mention the chase, only saying the man ran off when Arthur attempted to pursue. He described the man's wiry frame and flighty demeanour. Wilton nodded his way through the story.

"It sounds like this man was doing more than just issuing threats, wouldn't you say, sir?" Wilton said, finally.

"Yes. Perhaps so."

"Is there anything else you can tell me, sir?"

"There is," said Arthur. "I know his name. Alexander Frye."

. . .

After he had gone, Arthur explained everything to the others. Laura looked on, worried and even angry. Some deep, dark evil was at work, that she knew. What she didn't know, and what scared her most, was how all this was going to end.

Sophia, Jonathan and Mina decided to continue with their mission as planned.

For the next few hours, they were in God's hands. And each-others.

10th December – 5.30pm

The journey to the paper-mill was almost unbearably tense. No words had passed between them since stepping into the carriage. Arthur had provided that as well, though his crest had been removed from the doors, to prevent anything negative coming back onto him.

Sophia drove the carriage while Jonathan and Mina sat inside, holding hands as if it were a pleasant Sunday drive. The clip-clop of the horse's hooves provided a calming rhythm for them all. When the paper-mill came into view, Sophia signalled. Jonathan felt his wife's hand grip his tighter.

Sophia halted the horses a little distance away before jumping down onto the cobbled street. Jonathan and Mina stepped out, bracing themselves for the ordeal ahead.

Sophia had been eying the building closely. She turned to them both, with a grave look on her face.

"Something is wrong," she said finally. "The cart Frye was driving is gone."

. . .

They approached even more cautiously now, prepared for even more foul play. Jonathan recalled how sly Renfield could be in service of the Count, but Frye seemed so much different. More joyfully aggressive and violent. And probably more cunning.

They passed through the ruined gates, all of them feeling like they had entered a strange, barren world. A few steps more and they were almost at the entrance. All three of them strained to hear anything coming from within, but there was nothing, just a large black hole, deeper than an abyss, waiting to greet them. Jonathan held up his hand and signalled that he would go in first.

He went inside.

Only seconds passed, but they dragged like hours. Eventually, Jonathan called them inside. Mina hurried in, scanning the dim interior for any sign of Quincey. Or Frye. Or even the earth-box. But there was nothing.

"They are gone" said Jonathan.

Mina ran to him and he held her tight.

Sophia walked around the large space. There was an awful smell in the air, one which Jonathan and Mina knew well. The smell of decay and death. The kind of smell that infected the atmosphere everywhere the Count went. She began to recognise shapes in the dim light, humped shapes, like half-filled sacks, strewn across the floor. Five of them. There was also the tiniest noise that grew louder as she got nearer - the droning buzz of flies.

The shapes were bodies. Three male, two females. Pale and drained, they had been cast aside like broken toys. Sustenance, she knew, for Dracula. Sophia shuddered. One of the corpses seemed to be pointing. It's arm deliberately placed. She followed the slightly shrivelled hand and saw it was indeed pointing to the far wall.

"Jonathan! Mina!" she called, when she saw what was written there.

They ran over to her and followed her gaze to the wall. On it, written in blood, was a message –

See you tomorrow

Frye knew he was being followed. They cursed him more for his cunning and crafty nature. They had no idea if Dracula had already gone to St Katherine's Dock and boarded the *Groza*, or if he had another hiding place somewhere within the city.

As they stood together, helpless as to what to do next, they heard a sound. A low, quiet scraping sound, like nails on wood. The three of them tensed. Then that sound was accompanied by a feint rustle of movement.

They began to look about them, searching for the source of the noise. Sophia squinted into the gloom. Her eyes rested on the scattered bodies. One of them was moving.

Sophia alerted the others, pointing over towards the rumpled shapes. They could see one of them, it looked like a woman, struggling to its feet. Their first urge was to go and help. She was, after all, a victim of Dracula. But Sophia had looked at those bodies, and the aura of death was upon them all.

They heard a tiny squeal coming from above. Looking up, they saw a giant bat at one of the upper windows. Two tiny dots of red shone from its beady eyes. No doubt, this was Dracula, calling a new vampire to life.

Looking back at the figure, it shuffled forward toward them. The woman's face was pale, with a hint of sadness around the eyes. But the jaw was set firm and cruel.

"Be ready" whispered Jonathan.

No sooner had the words left his lips when the creature shot toward them, letting out a hideous cry. The mouth was open wide, revealing long, sharp teeth. The vampire moved swiftly toward Sophia, who was struggling to pull the crucifix from her pocket. The woman pushed Sophia to the floor, scrambling on top of her.

Jonathan had his kukri knife in his hands, and with a swift movement, he sliced viciously along the vampires back. The devil turned on him then, snarling and crouching like an animal, preparing to strike. As he held firm, waiting for the next attack, Sophia got to her feet, now holding the crucifix out in front of her. The vampire began to cower away from it. Mina joined her from the other side, holding her crucifix out like a shield. They formed a semi-circle around the figure, until she was cornered against one of the stone walls. She looked at the three of them with pure hatred and venom, swiping her long fingernails at them like a trapped tiger. As another snarl passed her lips, Jonathan plunged his knife into the vampire's chest.

The woman's body tensed for a moment, then relaxed, as a look of peace crossed her face. Jonathan caught her body as it slid down the wall, preventing a cruel fall to the floor. Instead, he rested it gently on the ground.

"There," he said. "She is at peace."

The bat gave out a horrific cry and flew off into the night on leathery wings. They ran out to see what direction it had flown, but the sky was empty.

…

Laura welcomed them home. She was smiling, but it seemed forced. Even that faded when she saw the defeat in their eyes. They ate together, for the sake of keeping up their strength and nothing else. After dinner, the three of them retreated to Jonathan and Mina's room.

"It's over then" she said.

"What do you mean, Mina?" asked her husband.

"We cannot stop him. There is no way to defeat him, don't you see?" Mina's tone was matter of fact.

"We will find a way!" Sophia interjected. "My Uncle, Christina… they will have died for nothing if we don't try!"

"No." Mina said. "I have resigned myself to the fact that in order to get our son back, I must give myself to Dracula."

"No! Never!" Jonathan leapt to his feet. "I will not allow it!"

Mina stood and approached her husband, taking his hand and kissing it. "It is alright, my love. It is a small price to pay to get our son back and for you and him to go on and live your lives together."

Tears began to crawl down Jonathan's face. "But… Mina…"

"He may have me, but he will not own my

soul Jonathan. I guarantee you that. Please, my husband, do not argue with me in this. Let it be."

He tried to speak but words would not come. They opened their arms to each other and embraced tightly.

Outside their room, Arthur listened at the door.

11th December – 9pm

The dock was deserted. Jonathan, Mina and Sophia stepped out of their carriage near the waterside. As they walked toward the *Groza,* their eyes flickered up toward the tall warehouses on their right, the dark windows looking down on them like judgmental faces, all of them asking – *how has it come to this?* There was no way out. There was nothing they could think of, nothing they could do, but surrender to the nightmare ahead. The *Groza* was the only large ship at port. The wood looked black in the moonlight, the masts pointing up into the night like spears, piercing the sky with stars.

The rest were only small boats, bobbing up and down on the river.

The water lapped peacefully against the hull and the gangplank creaked as the three of them boarded the ship. As promised, the crew was nowhere in sight. There were also no dock workers. There were only three other figures standing in wait on the deck. Frye stood with Quincey, casually dangling his knife over the boy's right shoulder, and holding Arthurs stolen revolver in his other hand. Quincey looked catatonic – hypnotised. Mina's heart leapt when she saw her son but tried her best not to betray her feelings. Her eagerness would only fuel the Count's sense of victory.

Standing next to them, his black robes wrapped around him like giant bat wings, was Dracula himself. He was smiling cruelly. He bowed mockingly.

"Welcome," he said. "I am glad you have done the sensible thing and come here. Surely by now you must know that I can never be stopped."

Mina stepped forward. "Give my son to me" she said. "And you can get what you want."

Dracula smiled again. "First, you will come to me, then I will release my hold over him."

She glanced at Jonathan, their hands touched, and tears began to well in her eyes. Jonathan's face showed heartbreak as his wife pulled away from him. Sophia watched helplessly, willing for a time, a chance, where she could turn the tide. As Mina approached Dracula, she turned and looked at her son. His eyes were fixed forward, not seeing or hearing. Frye smiled smugly at the inevitability of it all.

She was directly in front of Dracula now. The vampire turned to Frye and nodded. Frye pushed the boy gently forward, while the Count waved his hand slightly, directing Quincey towards his father's open arms.

Sophia gripped the crucifix in her pocket. Her other hand edged behind her toward the handle of the knife attached to her belt. Her eyes began to follow every movement of the figures around her, seeking a chance to avenge her Uncle. Quincey reached his father and Jonathan embraced him tightly, lifting the boy off his feet. Quincey shook his head lightly, as if waking from a dream.

"Quincey?" said Jonathan, worry in his voice.

"Father!" the boy exclaimed. He hugged Jonathan tightly.

Mina smiled. Regardless of anything else, her son was safe.

"Now you are mine," said Dracula imperiously, looking down at her, the red light of triumph in his eyes.

Suddenly, a shot rang out. The bullet seemed to sing as it flew towards its target, hitting Frye. None of them could see where the bullet struck him, they only saw a bloom of red as he fell sharply backwards onto the deck, the gun sliding from his grip, over the side and into the water below. Jonathan looked up towards the warehouse windows, trying to find the location of their saviour, and then he saw. It was Arthur. He was standing triumphantly, holding his hunting rifle in the air. He disappeared from the window like a phantom.

Dracula snarled viciously; the light of triumph turned to rage. Sophia leapt at him, pushing Mina protectively out of the way and brandishing Van Helsing's crucifix in his face. The silver metal pressed against the side of his face, burning it like hot iron. He screamed as the metal pulled away from his skin, leaving the mark of God branded in his searing flesh. He cowered back, lifting his cloak in front of his eyes. She drew the hunting knife, preparing to plunge it into Dracula's chest when he swiped at her violently, knocking her back onto the deck with a cruel thud.

Arthur appeared at the bottom of the gangplank. Jonathan ran to him.

"Give me Quincey," ordered Arthur. The boy had begun to wail.

Jonathan handed over his protesting son, kissing him on the forehead. "It will be alright," he said. "Go with Uncle Arthur."

Arthur took the boy in his arms. "He will be safe, I promise."

"Thank you," said Jonathan breathlessly. "For everything."

Arthur nodded and ran toward the warehouse, out of sight. Jonathan turned toward the fight and entered the fray. He saw Sophia lying on the deck and Mina moving backward, as Dracula pressed her to the rail. The vampire pressed his hand to the side of his face, trying to stem the pain. Pulling it away, he looked at his palm, covered with fragments of burnt flesh.

Drawing his kukri knife, Jonathan ran toward the vampire and sliced at his back. With a yelp of pain, Dracula turned and grabbed Jonathan by the throat, lifting him off his feet and throwing him like a rag doll. He tumbled as he hit the floor, the knife landing beneath him.

Mina ran to her husband, kneeling next to him. He was still breathing, barely conscious and groaning in pain. She covered him protectively. As she did so, she slipped her hand under Jonathan's body, grabbing the handle of the knife.

"I wanted him to live in torment for the rest of his days," hissed the Count, "knowing you were mine forever. But he will pay for this outrage. All of you. You will watch his heart stop beating when I rip it from his chest."

He walked over to her, grabbing her by the back of the neck and lifting her away from her husband, turning her bodily to face him. "You are mine."

Mina pushed the kukri knife with all her might, all her collected anger, sorrow and hate into Dracula's chest, as he had pushed the stake into Van Helsing's. The vampire staggered back, looking down at the hilt sticking out of his body. He started to reach for her, but she moved back away from him, leaving his arms flailing at air. She could see his skin starting to flake and crumble as destruction called for him once again.

"You will never rid yourself of me." He began to choke, as if the very words were turning to ash in his mouth. "My soul will call to you from hell."

With a final surge of anger, Mina pushed Dracula over the rail, his body tumbled down, his cloak spreading about him like wings, before exploding into dust as it hit the water. She saw the kukri knife sink beneath the waves as the Count's remains dissipated across the surface of the water, dissolving into nothing.

She smiled with relief for the first time in days. Then relief turned to agony as Frye stabbed her in the side. He had dragged himself over to her, the front of his shirt soaked in blood from the bullet wound in his shoulder. He screamed as he stabbed her again, his grief at the destruction of Dracula giving power to his vengeful act.

Jonathan had propped himself up on his elbows, just in time to see his wife stagger against the rail. The throbbing fog in his head cleared in an instant with an agonising wave of shock.

Frye stood up unsteadily, gripping the rail for support. He was going to use his knife again. Jonathan saw him raise the bloodied blade into the air as he tried to stand. Out of the corner of his eye, Jonathan saw movement. It was Sophia. She was up and moving like a streak of lightning, slashing the hunting knife across Frye's throat with a barbaric scream. He gurgled horribly, choking on the blood in his throat, pawing at the open wound as his body lurched over the rail and pitched into the water, joining his Master in death.

Jonathan stumbled over to his wife. He took her in his arms, her very life blood pouring from the wounds in her side, spreading warmly over him. He laid her gently on the ground, kneeling beside her.

"No," he cried over and over. "Mina, no."

She raised a delicate hand to his face and laid it on his cheek. "It's alright," she said. "You'll be alright."

"How will I live without you?" he said, tears flowing freely down his face.

"You will, because you must." She replied.

Sophia stood near them; her own face streaked with sorrow.

"Mother?"

They all looked toward the young voice. Quincey was there with Arthur. He ran to his parents, enveloping them both in a delicate embrace.

"My boy," said Mina softly. "My beautiful boy."

"Are you ill again, Mother?" he said,

innocently, not able to find any other words to express his feelings.

Mina smiled at him, her motherly love enveloping his sweet soul. "Mother will be feeling better soon" she said.

In his own way, Quincey seemed to understand what she meant. His eyes glistened wetly as he leant over and kissed her cheek. "Are you going to sleep now?" he asked.

"Yes," she replied. "I'm going to sleep now."

Mina turned toward her husband. He could see an aura of peace emanating from her eyes. The light of peace and tranquility that had been missing for so long had returned.

"Goodbye my love" she said, before closing those eyes forever.

12th December

The dawn had brought yet more death. Yet it had also brought salvation too.

Inspector Wilton had his men retrieve Alexander Frye's body from the river. He had also seen the Harker family, father and son, grief stricken and distraught. After interviewing Lord Godalming again, and a young lady named Sophia, the burned bodies at the Harker house had been identified and they all wept new tears for the fallen dead. Frye, it seemed, had also been responsible for that and for the kidnapping of the Harker's son.

No reason could be ascertained. Yet, if Frye were a madman, would any reason be necessary? The Inspector, through various other sources, had found out that Frye was a former inmate of an asylum in Durham. His former Doctor, now retired, recalled the curious case very well and was happy to speak about it. Their telephone conversation had been quite eye-opening.

Dock workers had been interviewed, all of them testifying that yes, the man known as Alexander Frye had paid them all in gold to leave the dock deserted for that night.

There was something else here, thought Wilton. Something he was not seeing. An extra layer of a mystery that nobody wanted to be solved. Why had Frye targeted them particularly? And where had he got all the gold from? It seemed to be foreign. Lord Godalming offered all the assistance he could in bringing the matter to a close. Wilton couldn't help but notice his eagerness for that to be the case.

The Inspector was never happy with open and shut cases. There was always something else, he thought. And there was certainly something else here. But dots could be joined, and numbers could be added up if that's what everyone wanted. And so, it seemed. This time, perhaps, a neat bow would have to do.

…

1905

15th August

My Dearest Mina,

Quincey has grown so much in the last months. Each day that passes, he reminds me more and more of you. Your radiance shines from his smile, his eyes. He suffered for a long while after what happened. Well, we all did. The grief was almost immeasurable. If anything, I think Quincey helped me more than I him, another thing which makes him so very much your son. You were always my rock, even when I was trying to be yours. He has many questions. I think perhaps, when he is a little older, I will show him our collected diaries and letters from all those years ago, and he can know the full truth of everything – not just of Dracula, but of your bravery.

There was so much chaos and mess to sort through. Arthur managed to smooth a great deal of it over through his contacts. I have a feeling he was owed a great many favours as Lord Godalming, all of which he collected. I do not want to use the word lucky, as that does not describe our situation at all, but serendipity was on our side. Mr Frye, it seemed, was a former resident of an asylum in Durham. While I know in my heart that this man had been possessed by Dracula's evil, his time there was able to fill many holes for the officers covering our case. A relapse back into insanity has been blamed for everything. Not an ideal situation, perhaps, but an uneasy line has been drawn under what happened. I made sure that our dear Christina and her fiancé were buried together. More innocent victims lost to Dracula's revenge. I am haunted by all that happened, and all we had to do to bring it to a close. The fire, especially, invades my dreams nightly. I get some idea now, my dear one, of all that you were going through. I hope God can forgive me.

Arthur is to be a father now. Laura is almost

due. It is a pleasure to see happiness once again in his face at the prospect of new life. I think he still blames himself for some of what happened at the end, but I have endeavoured to show him that is not the case. Evil in this world is very real and grief can become an ally or an enemy in our quest to fight it. For him, grief was both of those things.

We all visit Stephanie regularly. Her scars, like ours are not outside but in, and I don't think they will ever completely heal, but over time, I'm sure they will fade.

Sophia has decided to devote all her time to study. She is studying myths and legends around the world, specifically vampires. She tells me she intends to find the source of this terrible plague and stamp it out entirely. I believe that she can. A Van Helsing indeed. And she will always have an ally in me. Her actions that night hold a special place in my heart.

My life as a Solicitor carries on. Quincey

and I lived with Laura and Arthur for more than three months after you passed. We have our own house now and are working to make it a home.

We miss you, my dearest one, every hour of every day. But what keeps Quincey and I both going is the knowledge that you reside peacefully now in heaven, your soul free from Dracula's clutches.

Until we meet again, my darling.

All my love,

Jonathan.

...

Sitting in his new study, he put the pen down on his desk and looked over the letter once again. Satisfied, he folded it and placed it in an envelope.

...

Strolling through the cemetery, his son at his side, they stopped when they reached Mina's grave. Quincey was holding a small bunch of wildflowers that he placed reverently at the base of the headstone. As the birds sung and the sun shone brightly through the trees, Jonathan placed the envelope amongst the flowers. They stood for a few moments, silence saying more than words. Then he took his son's hand and they began to walk slowly away.

"So," said Jonathan, smiling. "What shall we do today?"

ABOUT THE AUTHOR

Starting out as a playwright, Damian has written more than twelve one-act, full-length and short plays and sketches for both adults and children – all available on www.lazybeescripts.co.uk. As a fan of the Dracula character, he has long wanted to write a sequel to the original novel, so what you have just read represents a lifelong ambition.

Printed in Great Britain
by Amazon